Mattie & the Yellow Dress

By Scott Cuffe

Mattie & the Yellow Dress

By Scott Cuffe
Copyright 2018
All Rights Reserved
ISBN: 978-1-387-56068-4

Forward

Chapter 1
Mattie & the Yellow Dress

Chapter 2
The Aftermath

Chapter 3
Taking Care of Business

Chapter 4
Dinner & Counseling

Chapter 5
Chit Chat

Chapter 6
The Party

Chapter 7
30 Years Later…

Chapter 8
Mattie's Diary

Forward

I fought to not wake up from my dream that Sunday morning. I don't remember ever doing that before, I have not *wanted* to wake up because of a great dream, but never have I *fought* to not wake up. I fought with every ounce of my being; at least my mind's being, since my body lay asleep.

And I slept another hour or two, until my dream story was complete. I woke up, ran to my clipboard with paper and red pen and began writing down this story. This has been my habit for years, that way I don't forget the story, the dream or any of its details.

So that Sunday morning, I made coffee and sat down at my computer and wrote the first chapter of this novella. 8 hours later it was edited and done. And I was happy. Ecstatic is a better way to describe myself, even thrilled beyond belief.

Then over the next 6 days I did the same thing every night, as I went to bed I asked God to give me the next chapter. The next morning I awoke, the chapter complete in my mind and I sat at my computer for 8-10 hours that day and when I was done the chapter was edited and completed and added to the previous day's work. One chapter a day until I had 7 chapters and I felt the novella was done. Two of those days I never ate anything all day, but I didn't notice. I was so very happy to write this story, my dream of hope and peace.

Those of you who know me and have read my non-fiction book entitled, "Arizona Cop Stories" know the struggles and damage I endured during my 20 years as a police officer. In those 30 short stories from my career, I tried to explain the horror, the damage and the madness that was never ending for me and my brothers and sisters in arms in our war against evil. To this day, 9 years after retirement, the pain and suffering is still with me and it has left me with no hope of a future or salvation. I had given up on finding peace and love and for my nightmares to end.

Until I dreamed this story. In this book, I found the answers I have been seeking for almost 30 years.

The seven days in a row that I wrote this novella, I have never felt that way in my life before. It was an epiphany moment for sure, a true one, one that I had been searching to find for so long. I feel that my soul or guardian angel, or if they are one and the same, finally gave me this dream to save me.

P. S., I wrote the 8th and final chapter two months later; after another dream and it makes the novella more complete and fills in many gaps. Uniquely for me, I tried to write it from a woman's voice, so see if you can tell if I wrote the entire book or a woman wrote the last chapter.

P. P. S., as *time* in dreams seldom matters or is hard to track, see if you as the reader can follow the time/day of the week sequence of this novella and at the end of it tell how many days have elapsed or passed by…does this prove my novella is a dream? *Hint*: Each chapter does not equal one day.

This story explains how a cop's soul can be destroyed by doing the job and how the passage of time can make some of the demons disappear. It also shows how love of a caring person can make life better and how holding a hand and being loved can chase the nightmares away forever.

Author Scott Cuffe circa 2000

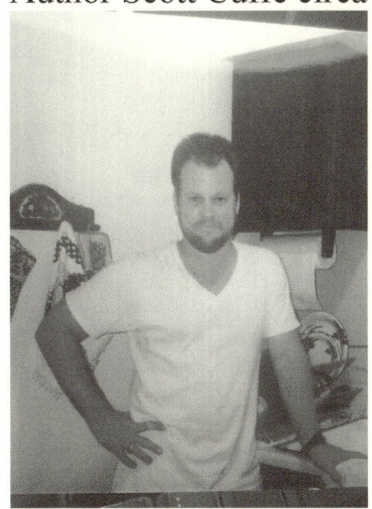

circa 2017

Chapter 1
Mattie & the Yellow Dress
Day 1

    It was about 6 am in the morning as I drove northbound on I-25 north of Hatch, New Mexico. Off in the distance I could see what appeared to be smoke, lots of it, and I soon realized it was a huge out of control grassland wildfire. As I got closer I saw many stopped vehicles, some turning around to go the way we came and then a couple fire trucks and cop cars arrived and turned all of us back. We were not going north on I-25 this morning so we had to find an alternate route.

    As it is I figure, when one turn goes away and you are forced to take another, one you would never take on your own, good things can happen. So as I drove back to Hatch and then on highway 26 in a northbound roundabout way, I ended up in a small town called Hillsboro. It was about 7:45 am and I saw a breakfast restaurant and parked in front.

    Once inside, a man was cooking in the kitchen and a waitress came over and poured me coffee and two old guys were sitting in a corner booth, one that I am sure has been their spot for the last 40 years. I noticed before I came into the restaurant that the town looked like it was about ready to have some kind of street fair or carnival or the like. I asked my waitress and she said in three days it was their annual festival or fair called the "Love, Peace and Friendship Fair." The fair was started some 80 years ago by locals.

She then asked me, "Can you use any of that?"
"Absolutely, exactly what I'm looking for in fact," I responded.

"Then stick around a couple days, I'm sure a big guy like you can lend a helping hand," she said.

"Who do I ask to help?" I requested.

"Mattie is her name and here she comes now," the waitress said.

I looked out the window and watched as a woman, 5 foot 6 inches tall, 122 pounds, short brown hair, wearing blue jeans and a button up long sleeve western shirt, half unbuttoned to show her ample chest, walked in. The waitress spoke to her and pointed at me and this beautiful woman walked over to me.

"What do you want?" She asked politely.

"I just wanted to see if your eyes matched the rest of you," I stated.

She laughed out loud and said, "No really, Carol said you wanted to help out with our fair?" She countered.

"Now that I have seen your eyes, I sure do," I laughed back.

"You are a stranger, why would you want to help us?"

"I am a wanderer and I help people wherever I can," I stated as I pulled out my wallet and showed her my retired police officer badge.

"Why are you showing me this?" She asked.

"Just to show you I didn't work as a cop for 20 years helping people to turn into a weirdo after I retired."

She told me after I finished my breakfast to come find her down in all the hustle and bustle of the fair set-up area, which was at the end of town on Main Street (the only street as far as I could tell).

"I want to thank you in advance for letting me help and attend the fair," I told her.

"You are a weirdo after all," she said laughing as she grabbed her coffee.

"Nice car, how'd you get the motorcycle on the back of that?" She asked but didn't wait for my answer before she walked out the door.

She looked as gorgeous walking away as she did walking in.

Besides not being a weirdo, let me describe myself: five foot 11 inches, 200 pounds, low body fat, lift weights 6 days a week, 90 minutes of aerobics 6 days a week, fit as fiddle. Big arms, lots of muscles, able to lift very heavy stuff, fight pretty good, crack shot, enemy of the bad guy, or at least I used to be. Good looking, not ugly and I love to laugh and sunsets, beaches (well not beaches really) but it sounds good. And smart, let me not forget smart.

Oh, and I like to wear v-neck white t-shirts. Really bright white ones. And blue jeans and I drive a white VW beetle with an old, antique cherried-out awesome 1971 Honda CB350 motorcycle strapped on the back of my Beetle. The Beetle gets me places and the motorcycle is for short drives when I'm there.

After breakfast I drove down to the end of the street and parked. Lots of human activity--like ants on a hill.

I walked over and was on the receiving end of lots of stares, but used to that from 20 years of being a cop. Mattie and I saw each other about the same time, she rolled her eyes and we walked to meet each other.

"I didn't think you would show up," she stated.

"Glad to be here," I responded.

"Weirdo," she muttered quietly.

"Heavy lifting is my specialty," I stated. And she sent me over to help some guys with moving car tires from one side of the street to the other side to be lined out for a driving track for go-carts. Once there instead of carrying them all (about 150 tires) I suggested that I roll them across the street to the 4-5 guys who would grab one and set it in place and as they moved around the track I would roll the tires to them there. Basically they were forming two circles, one little one inside the larger outer circle of tires and the kids would drive the go-carts between them.

We all agreed and we set up our positions and for the next 90 minutes, I rolled tires all over the place. Most made their target but once in a while a tire had a mind of its own and went haywire and we laughed out loud many a time. But overall the system worked and I was sweaty and exhausted and so were the other guys, but they said it shaved an hour or two off the normal set-up time.

Next I helped the crew bring in a bunch of porta potties and Thank God they were empty or we would all have been quarantined forever the way they tipped over so easily and we fumbled around with them. Potty jokes flew freely as we worked on this task, and again, thank goodness they were empty. I told them I would be busy at the end of the fair when they had to be loaded up full.

Once in awhile I looked up and saw Mattie smiling and not rolling her eyes anymore.

Next came the herculean task of setting up their famous 80 year old Ferris wheel. It was made of wood, even the baskets, and it consisted of two huge beams joined at the top forming an upside down "V" and then a cross member beam about shoulder height going horizontal to attach to both of those beams on each end. The beams were attached with big metal plates that holes drilled through them and the beams and were joined by large bolts. There was one of these on each side of the wheel which contained just 4 baskets which held two adults or three kids each. The entire

Ferris wheel was about 20 foot tall I would guess, but very heavy because of the wood it was made from and decades of aging.

And so it went this first day, this day one in this no stop light town in New Mexico. The men folk were busy the women folk were busy and the kids either helped or played, and both were good. I saw no fighting or arguing about setups or places for stuff or arrangements or decorations. I saw family and friends taking care of business with love peace and friendship…they had a good name for their fair, a good one indeed.

It was getting dark and a few of the men wanted to test some of their older fireworks and did so as a couple ladies came up to me to feed me. They sat me down and one brought me an ice cold beer and another a plate of soft tacos with rice and beans. I had no food since breakfast and it was a long hard working day and I relished the food and drink.

Mattie stopped by and asked if she could join me at my table.

"I thank you in advance if you would," I responded.

"What the heck does that even mean??" She asked almost crazily.

"I don't ever want to forget to thank someone for something they did for me or not get the chance to thank them, so I do it in advance," I told her.

"That's almost crazy, at best backwards," she described.

"For 20 years I had to live that way, expecting each work day to be my last. I lived death too much to not know I could be next. I heard over and over for those years--the survivors who wished they would have said more to the deceased person while they were alive. So I learned to be thankful and appreciative and do it in advance."

"Have another beer," she said as she handed me her bottle to swig from and she got up to get us two more.

When she returned I asked her to talk about her for me and at first she was reluctant to tell the weirdo retired cop anything but then she told me of a great life, always living here and becoming a nurse and returning to work for the one doctor in town. She regaled on the happiness of helping deliver babies and then watching the kids grow, how helping people was what she was meant to do. She loved her family and friends and they her.

I asked her why everyone seemed to love her so much, and she asked how I could tell and I told her, "I'm a trained observer." She said it was that way for everyone here, not just her. "How wonderful that must be," I said quietly to myself, but she heard me.

Mattie then asked me to grab a set of clean clothes for tomorrow and I asked why and she asked if I had a place to sleep tonight and I told her I didn't have time to look and she said her spare bedroom would suit me just fine. I walked over and grabbed some clean clothes from the trusty VW Beetle. Upon my return she laughed at my small yellow night bag that held my clean clothes. She asked why the yellow color and I told her it was my favorite happy color and that, "It made my slumped soul sit up straight."

Exhausted and sweaty and dusty and dirty, she took me to the two-room community bathhouse (never heard of such a thing but loved the idea) across the street from her house, and went in with me on one side and locked the door. Along one wall was a very large shower room, about 8 feet by 10 foot with three different shower heads inside. One was lower and made for a wheelchair person. I told her they really thought ahead and made an awesome community bathhouse building. Along another wall were a washer and clothes dryer and a long skinny table for folding clothes. Along the third wall were a double sink and two stool stalls for bathroom use.

"Give me your dirty clothes," Mattie demanded in a soft way.

"I will wash them while you are taking a shower."

Mattie made no attempt to turn her vision away from me or move her legs in order to walk somewhere else, so I did what was natural. I undressed in front of her, walked over to her and handed her my dirty clothes. She laughed at my red underwear, but never took her gaze off me. I walked over to the shower and the water felt so good.

When I got out of the shower she handed me a towel and my clean clothes. She said she would finish my dirty clothes later and we walked across the street to her house.

Mattie had Tequila and some tortilla chips and salsa in case we were hungry. After about an hour of tequila and talking we were both exhausted and she showed me off to her spare bedroom.

Day 2

I awoke to a knock on the spare bedroom door and in came Mattie carrying a cup of joe for me.

"Morning sunshine," she yelled softly.

"Good morning to you!" I answered back.

She came over to hand me the cup of coffee and leaned over the bed and kissed me tenderly.

"Wow! I wish every morning was like this," I cooed.

"It could be…who knows," she answered.

"Well, I thank you in advance if it turns out to be true." We both laughed.

"Can we talk for awhile before we get back to the grind?" Mattie asked me.

"Sure, I would love to," I answered.

"Tell me why you are a wanderer?"

There was silence for a short time.

"In my life, my career as a cop, those 20 years took their toll on me. I have seen too much suffering, too much death, hatred, too much pain and loss. And even though I told myself my pain is 1% of the pain a victim feels, I have suffered thousands of those one percent experiences and they added up."

"I trained myself during those years, sort of like meditation, to free my mind. More like emptying my mind, and better yet learning to think of nothing." I explained further. "Imagine sitting for an hour or two or more, thinking of nothing. Not a single thought about anything filling your head. I was always aware of my surroundings, sight, smell, hearing and the like, but I could think of nothing. No pain, no happiness, no nothing."

"Now that I am retired and older, I lost that ability. Without this ability to zone out, the nightmares are always present. Sleep, rest and of course peace are not abundant in my life."

"I don't know why, I was real good at it for 20 years, but I find I can't do it anymore now that I am no longer doing the job. I wish I could, but I can't, so I came up with another solution to help me—travel, wander and find good people being nice to each other."

"How has that worked for you so far?" she asked.

"Not as well as I had hoped," I said.

"Maybe peace and happiness are not in my future," I sadly explained.

"Nonsense! Today I will guarantee you lots of happiness and peace and corn dogs and monkey on a stick from the food vendors if you want it...hahahahaha!" She cried out happily.

So off we went to the fair. Busy were all the people setting up their booths and decorations. I saw a group of men standing by three trucks full of lumber and walked over to offer my help. The truckload of wood was 2 x 4 lumber all predrilled and numbered for the construction of each booth. Bolts held them all together and it made it easier to set up and take down each year of the fair. I told them I could lift heavy stuff and I began a many hour task of unloading the wood from the trucks, carrying them over to the designated spaces--thus freeing the men to work on setting up the booths themselves. Before long a row of booths stood erect and ready for decorating and signage to be put on them. I saw the sign "Meat on a Stick" and its booth and figured that was the origin of Mattie's "Monkey on a stick" comment.

Everyone toiled for about 8 hours and finally the fair was done, all decorated and very beautiful and ready for tomorrow. It was about 5 pm and we still had a couple of hours left of daylight so I asked Mattie if she thought the kids would like to take rides on my motorcycle.

"Are you kidding? They would love it!" She explained. So as I was unloading my motorcycle, Mattie was lining up the kids and making sure they had their parent's permission.

One by one for about 2 hours, every kid and even some men and ladies got to ride on the back of my motorcycle up and down Main Street, always doing only about 20 mph or less. Every time I looked Mattie's way, she was smiling and seemed very happy. Some kids wanted to go 100 mph, but I never gave in.

My white t-shirt was beyond dirty and dusty and sweaty from this long day. Mattie was my last rider and I asked her if we could go on a longer ride, to which she said yes immediately, and then I apologized she had to hold onto my sticky sweaty dirty t-shirt and body.

"What is it with you and clean white t-shirts?" She asked me.

"I have never made it to the end of a day with a clean t-shirt, something always happens to prevent it, in fact I usually carry an extra clean shirt in my car wherever I go," I explained.

"I don't mind at all!" she answered.

And of course she looked as fresh and gorgeous as the first time I saw her that morning.

"How do you do it?" I asked her.

"Do what?" she queried.

"Look so gorgeous?" I said.

"I'm a princess, didn't you now?" She stated matter-of-factly.

"That explains why everyone loves you so much, I get it now."

We were both laughing as we drove off for a nice sunset ride away from the town.

About an hour later I pulled up to her house and she went inside. I grabbed some clean clothes out of the VW Bug and walked into her house. She called me from her bathroom and I went in.

This time as she told me to give her my dirty clothes to put in the washing machine, she already had hers off.

"I'm taking a shower with you tonight if that's okay?" she said.

"I want to thank you in advance," I responded excitedly.

Hours later, the last thing I remember that evening was holding her hand before I passed out in her bed.

Day 3

The next morning, in that cloud of softness that is her bed, floating and 8 hours later I awoke. I realized I was alone in the bed but quickly noticed as Mattie walked up to me, kissed me tenderly and handed me a cup of joe.

"Good morning beautiful," I said to her and she smiled back.

"Did you have any bad dreams last night?"

"No, just of you and floating in a cloud."

"Hahahaha," she murmured.

"Big day today, you ready for it?"

"I sure am and thank you for the coffee."

"You are welcome," she answered.

We ate the most wonderful breakfast she prepared, huevos ranchero, fried eggs on top of hot corn tortillas with lots of salsa, Mattie's famous salsa, with some rice and her coffee was to kill for.

"Why did you make breakfast? With all the food that will be at the fair today?" I asked.

"Because this morning is a special morning and I wanted to make it for you."

"Well thank you, it was delicious!"

She leaned over the table and we kissed, a soft, long kiss, full of peace and love.

"And I have another surprise for you, I'll be right back, now get dressed!"

I put on my fresh clean clothes, and I noticed she picked out a superb example of my white v-neck t-shirts, probably the whitest and best one I own.

A few minutes later she told me to turn around and once I did my eyes were as pleased as was my soul. She was wearing the most beautiful bright yellow dress I have ever seen in my life. She could tell it made me happy by my smile from ear to ear and I thanked her again.

"What for?" she asked.

"For making my soul sit up straight from its slumped position."

She walked over and kissed me and then hugged me for eternity. I never wanted to let her go.

"Let's go, busy day ahead!" She exclaimed and off we went.

The fair was bustling with workers, finishing up final touches here and there, filling the food booths, testing equipment and everything necessary to be ready for the 12 noon opening. This day would have the one day fair open from noon until 10:00 pm, ending with a small fireworks show. The fair usually had a couple hundred visitors throughout the day Mattie told me.

We both noticed a few of the men standing around and touching one leg of the Ferris wheel. They seemed concerned about something, so we walked over.

"Good morning!" Mattie yelled out. "Good morning," rang the chorus of response.

"What going on?"

"Joe accidentally backed up his ice truck this morning and rear ended into this leg of the Ferris wheel and we are checking for damage."

We looked also and saw nothing out of place.

"We are going to run the Ferris wheel empty for awhile to make sure everything is okay."

"Great idea," Mattie answered.

Mattie and I then walked to every single vendor, booth and ride at the fair, she was good at being in charge and everyone loved and respected her. Besides some minor issues of people waking up late, or some of the food being eaten by some kids or adults, everything seemed ready for the grand opening at noon.

"So far so good for your white t-shirt," she whispered softly to me in the crowd. As we walked around the fair, ladies and men kept coming up to us and hugging Mattie and shaking my hand.

"Like we were royalty," she said.

"I think they are just happy for you, they care for you so much."

"No, I am a princess, hahahahaha," she explained.

The opening came and went and everyone was happy and dancing in the street and singing with tons of kids running around all over the place, giggling could be heard everywhere, the men folk were clustered together, perhaps making up for lost time.

Hugs and handshakes and laughter were all around us. I felt like I was in a magical world with the most beautiful woman in all the land. Mattie's yellow dress was so very beautiful, she was stunning and I started to feel a little awkward in my stupid white t-shirt. I told her I was going to go change it for a nice button down shirt and she said not to. She liked her knight in white shining armor she said, she liked me just the way I was.

Mattie squeezed my hand even tighter as we walked around and enjoyed the fair. We visited everyone I am sure, ate well, laughed too much; I told her I would not have to do sit-ups for a week at least.

Being with her, seeing the life in her, it was amazing! I thought, I haven't felt this way in so many years, if ever. I tried to remember and couldn't. I thought how lucky I was that the grassland fire had forced me this way and into her world.

Then it all changed. Just like it did all those years as a cop. Something always came up to stop the joy and the magic and today turned out no different.

We heard screaming. Then more screaming. It was over by the little Ferris wheel. We ran over, I will never forget the yellow dress flowing as Mattie ran beside me. We got there and the Ferris wheel was stopped, with all four baskets full of three kids each and it was leaning to one side. I could see a large crack near the steel bracket plate on the leg where the ice truck backed into it. Men were trying to brace the horizontal beam up, to keep the leg from falling completely but only had some 2 x 4 boards, they were too long, and someone ran to get a saw to cut them down to size, but I knew they would not be strong enough. One man said to drive a car under the beam, but that would not work because it was not high enough and once the beam started to fall 3 or 4 feet down it would not stop when it hit the car and the Ferris wheel would still tumble over.

I grabbed Mattie by both shoulders. I kissed her softly.

"Listen to me carefully. First, get everyone away from the Ferris wheel to save as many people as possible. Second, unload the children from the Ferris wheel as normal. Do not go faster than normal because it may jerk the Ferris wheel and cause it to collapse sooner. And third, empty the east parking lot of all the people and if time permits--all the cars that could be crushed by the falling Ferris wheel."

"Okay, I got it but what are you going to do?" She asked me.

"I am going to give you time to do all the rest," I answered her.

Mattie ran off to do what I asked and what I knew she could do. I walked over and told a few of the men to get away from the Ferris wheel and evacuate all their families and friends to a safe distance. They all ran to do just that.

I told a couple of the men to help unload the children from the baskets of the Ferris wheel when the time came and to get them to safety.

I then walked under the cross horizontal wood beam, as close to the steel brackets and the broken leg as possible, but not touching them. I thanked God that this beam was my shoulder height, got under it and stood straight up to become the fourth leg of the Ferris wheel.

I thought of my happy soul and that yellow dress.

I couldn't move the beam up or straighten out the tilting Ferris wheel, but I could prevent it from tilting more and falling down any further. I knew I could keep it from collapsing for a minute or two, just long enough to help save the children.

If there was pain to my shoulders or body, I didn't feel any.

Mattie's eyes were full of terror when she saw what I had done but she knew she had to continue her life saving duties I laid out for her to accomplish. The fair was very busy with people moving all about and I assume loud, but I only heard silence.

In what I figured was to be my last minute or two in this world, I could see everything that was going on…the food booths next to the Ferris wheel were evacuated of people, people were helping people all around to get far away from the Ferris wheel, cars were being moved to safe distances in the dirt parking lot to the east.

The Ferris wheel was being unloaded of its children, one basket at a time. As it turned it lurched and creaked and moaned and wanted to fall down. I felt great pressure on my shoulders but no pain. I thought, this is why I worked out during my life, for this moment and I was not going to fail.

I have always been prepared to die. After 20 years of thinking every single day I went to work that that day could be the day I died, I was always ready. I was ready now. There was no fear.

In that minute or two, everything came together. The parking lot was emptied of its people and cars and all the people were far enough away from the danger as the last basket of children was unloaded off the Ferris wheel. So many heroes saving others, it was cool to observe.

Mattie, crying, started to walk closer to me and I held up my left hand, motioned and told her to stop and get back to a safe distance.

I told her softly, "I hoped today was the day I would make it to the end with a clean t-shirt."

She cried even more.

"Mattie, thank you for everything. I am so very glad to have met you. Thank you for wearing that gorgeous yellow dress for me, it gave my soul strength for this today…I love you Mattie."

And I stepped back and let go.

The Ferris wheel collapsed just as I thought; it followed the broken leg and fell eastward into the now empty dirt parking lot. Dust was kicked up by its collapse, so much so that nothing could be seen in almost the whole area of the fair.

People that were far enough away in safety of the Ferris wheel itself were not far enough from the dust it kicked up. The whole town was coughing and protecting their eyes.

Just as the dust was settling down I walked out of the ruble toward Mattie, somehow not killed by the falling debris of the collapsing Ferris wheel but dusty and dirty and bleeding from my right shoulder. I was dizzy and my vision was foggy and I simply walked towards the yellow dress and fell down never reaching it.

Day 4

That is the last thing I remember until the next afternoon when I awoke in a cloud. I thought I was dead and heaven was full of clouds, so I must be there. A few people in the room quickly made me understand that I was not in heaven, but in Mattie's bed.

Mattie came running into the room at all the commotion and ran up to me and kissed me long and hard and squeezed me and hugged me as hard as she could.

"Mattie, hello beautiful!" I exclaimed.

"Hello!" She responded softly.

"Did you have any bad dreams?" She asked me.

"No, just of you and floating in a cloud," I said to her.

We embraced each other in silence for a moment and then she said sobbingly, "I will give you love and peace for the rest of your life if you want it," and she squeezed me even harder.

"I want that more than anything and I thank you in advance."

Chapter 2
The Aftermath

My body felt great except for some soreness in my right shoulder where the Doc had to put in a few stitches to sew up skin that split on the top of it.

"A few stitches??!!" Mattie exclaimed quietly.

"How about 32 stitches to be exact and you just lie your butt back down in that cloud of mine mister!" She said in a half quiet voice.

"I've never been yelled at or scolded in a quiet voice before, I like it," I bemused out loud and slid back down into her bed.

"Let me take care of you for few days, then you can get up, but heal first, listen to your nurse!" she exclaimed again, this time a little louder.

Just then the Doc stopped by to check in on his patient. Doc Sanchez was a lean man, tall and with a dark thick mustache, thick glasses and a great bedside manner.

"Hold up any more impossibly heavy objects today?" He stated dryly.

"It wasn't that heavy," I stated calmly.

Mattie turned and shook her finger at me.

"How are you feeling Scott?" The Doc asked me.

"Ready to get out of bed, but my warden, my loving warden, won't let me."

Mattie shook two fingers at me this time.

"Seriously Doc, just a little sore on my right shoulder down to my waist. Feels like ribs are broken or something," I told him. "But other than that and the stitches are itchy, I feel great and I have the most beautiful nurse in the world and she likes me I think."

"Well I have your x-rays here and your ribs are not broken, they should be, in fact you should be dead. Nothing broken in your shoulder, amazing, and nothing wrong with your hips, your knees or anywhere I can see. Time will tell me if you have any ligament or cartilage damage, but as for now I don't even see any pulled muscles."

Mattie was hanging on Doc's every word and I could see she was worried. Funny I thought, she has only known me for a few days but she was already worried about me. I've never been on the receiving end like this before.

"Well Doc," I stated plainly, "All I did was stand there like a stump. I didn't lift anything and if that darn post hadn't hit my shoulder on my way down to the ground, I wouldn't have needed all these stitches."

He said, "From what I understand, you did a little bit more than that."

"Everyone did a little bit more than that Doc, I saw a lot of heroes that day, especially Mattie," I proclaimed. Mattie smiled at me.

"I have a friend of mine, a psychologist who has offered to come to our town to help with trauma counseling. She will be here tomorrow evening at the auditorium. She said she would give you and Mattie some private sessions if you want," the Doc told us.

I have done plenty of this during my cop career, was even a peer counselor for cops after stressful situations happened to them, so I know they can help, but I didn't need it.

However, I looked over at Mattie and I told the Doc, "You bet! Mattie and I would love some private sessions." Mattie looked at me and nodded approval.

"Mattie, the dressing on Scott's shoulder looks great, change it often, let me know if any infection or other problems come up and I will see you both tomorrow evening at the auditorium," the Doc said.

Doc left Mattie's home and she looked relieved, tremendously relieved.

"Can you come over here and sit close to me?" I asked Mattie.

She gladly walked over and I grabbed her hand and I asked, "How are you doing?"

"I have been so worried about you Scott. I watched you die and yet here you are," she said in a frail voice.

"But I didn't die and you know why?" I asked her as I squeezed her hands in mine.

"Because it was not my time, maybe I have suffered enough in my life and God is going to give me peace and love and a woman named Mattie to be my friend."

She began crying and laughing at the same time, "You are so corny sometimes!" And she grabbed me and hugged me so very hard.

The doorbell rang.

In came a host of people all carrying cooked dishes and bottles of wine and tequila and snacks of all sorts it seemed. Mattie was getting hugs and she told everyone to not shake my hand or hug me because of all the stitches, but a little kid or two snuck by her and gave me a hug anyway, which I enjoyed.

Everyone was pleasant and shared their concern for me and Mattie and said they would take care of tearing down the fair and putting everything back in storage so that Mattie could care for me.

They didn't stay more than 20 minutes and after many more hugs they were gone. She said to get used to it, because the town would be doing it until I was back on my feet and recovered.

"Well in case we don't like their food, I better get well quick!" I stated.

"You will love their food, just like I do," she scolded me and again quietly.

"You have the greatest bedside manner I have ever seen Mattie," I said. And she went over to the door, locked it, closed the curtains and by the time she got back to the bed her top was off.

"You haven't seen anything yet!" She exclaimed as she slid into the bed beside me.

That night was painful for me. I didn't want to wake Mattie to tell her and so I suffered quietly. Mattie was sleeping so calmly and peaceful and I wanted her to rest. Morning came early it seemed and she awoke rested and smiling.

"How are you feeling this morning Scott?" She asked me and she gave me a hug.

"It was a long painful night and I think I want to go for a walk to loosen up a bit if you care to join me," I told her.

"Why didn't you wake me up?" She scolded, again quietly.

"You were sleeping so peacefully and there was nothing you could have done to help my pain anyway. And I was taking care of you for a change," and I kissed her softly and sweetly.

We both dressed and were out the door for a walk about the town. It was early and cool outside with only the diner open with a few customers. The fair was about half taken down by the townsfolk and we strolled up one side of the street on a very nice sidewalk and I got my first real look at the town.

It was a beautiful one main street town and now I could see some side streets that I didn't know were there. The houses on these streets were beautiful and well kept and the businesses along Main Street were all clean and orderly and the storefronts looked well aged.

"We have everything we need here," Mattie said.

"I have everything I need right here," I said as I squeezed her soft hand in mine. She smiled and gave me a kiss on the cheek.

"Are you ready for the meeting tonight?" I asked Mattie.

"Yes, I look forward to it," she said.

"I'm going to open with remarks, I called Doc and he said it would be okay. He didn't know how many of the townsfolk would be receptive to outside trauma counseling and I told him I would help get them in the right mind for it."

"What are you going to talk about?" She asked.

"About heroes like you and the others and how you don't have to go it alone."

"I'm not a hero because of this," Mattie stated.

"Listen to my definition of a hero tonight and then decide if you are or not," I told her and squeezed her hand some more.

"My parents should be back in town tonight in time for the meeting. I told them all about the incident and about you."

"The shower part with me?" I exclaimed.

"No, not that part, but they know you are staying with me and I am a grown woman and get to make my own choices and they respect that," she said.

"Is your dad bigger than me or have more guns?" I queried.

"Hahaha, you are safe, trust me."

"My life is in your hands."

"Speaking of guns, do you have any with you?"

"Why do you ask?"

Because the townsfolk moved your car and motorcycle to my covered carport and I just realized there may be a gun inside of them."

"No one can gain access to my handgun, it is locked safe and secure and only I can get to it," I explained.

"Okay, I won't worry then," she said.

We walked to the end of Main Street and realizing the walk definitely helped my pain and stiffness, we returned back to Mattie's House.

We sat on her couch, holding hands and we talked for hours it seemed. Laughing and questioning each other, many of those things new couples do before they sleep together. Stuff to get to know each other better, belief systems, likes and dislikes and favorite colors and foods.

We ate a wonderful lunch from all the donated food people brought us and took a short nap together, spooning and cuddling and kissing her neck until we both fell asleep. It was very peaceful.

When we awoke we had just enough time to get dressed properly and walk over to the auditorium for the evening trauma counseling.

Once there, I met with the Doc and his doctor friend who was going to run the meeting. Doctor Snyder was very pleasant and said she was amazed after reading all the reports made on the incident.

"You are lucky to be alive," she told me.

"We are all lucky to be alive, it was a great team effort," I answered back to her.

The meeting came to order and Doc got up on stage and addressed the 100 or so townspeople who were in attendance. He introduced me as the opening speaker and I went up on stage and delivered the following message:

"Welcome to everyone that is here tonight. My name is Scott in case some of you haven't heard by now (laughter in the audience) and I want to say a few words to you all before the two Doctors take over to help us all deal with our trauma from the incident.

Since the incident, I have analyzed every single action of mine taken that evening and every single action taken by all of you, at least the ones I witnessed myself, and I have pieced the others together like I would at any crime scene I have ever worked. In case any of you don't know, I was a cop for 20 years in Arizona and am now retired (laughter again)."

"In this incident, this potentially deadly incident, I was amazed at how wonderful all the people of this town were as well as our out of town fair visitors. Everywhere I looked were people taking care of each other, helping each other to get to the right places, moving cars at great risk, taking children out of baskets and evacuating the fair grounds, when at any moment the Ferris wheel could have collapsed. I saw no one not doing something to save another person."

"You are all to be commended for your life saving actions that evening. You are to be proud of yourselves and your family, friends and neighbors. Now it is up to us to carry on and make life as best we can not only for ourselves but for everyone around us. But from what Mattie tells me, this town is expert at this already. Everyone in this auditorium is a hero, a life saver and I am lucky to have been there with all of you."

"Now please, let me tell you about Mattie. It was the combination of her nursing skills and experiences, her natural born leadership skills and the wonderful person that she is that enabled her to shine in this incident. Rarely have I been in such a chaotic situation and saw someone with nerves of steel like I did that evening with Mattie."

"As I stood there like a stump, a log holding up my end of the Ferris wheel, I was lucky enough to be able to witness this amazing woman at work and watch her actions save lives."

"I watched as she calmly approached people, gave them simple instructions and they ran off to accomplish it. Evacuation of the food booths, or fair grounds, moving cars to prevent them from being crushed, taking children out of the Ferris wheel baskets as the kids came around, I got to see it all, I had the best seat in the house."

"I was prepared to die that evening. I was not afraid. I have cheated death too many times before and know that I will not escape this life alive. I was calm. But I found that I was something more...I was proud. Of all the townspeople who were heroes in front of me and I was very proud of Mattie. Not because she likes me and gives me a kiss once in a while (the crowd laughs) but because she is a hero. A hero to everyone in this town and especially a hero to me."

"Mattie never stopped moving and directing people and coordinating the mass event, all with the simple goal of no one being killed or injured. In my career I have met too few highly trained men or women that could do such a thing. Well, Mattie can and did."

"When she first saw me go under the horizontal wood beam and stand there to brace it from falling; I saw the terror in her eyes. She would have given anything in this world to run over to me, grab me and pull me away from that Ferris wheel, but she turned and continued on with all her life saving directions and coordination of all you amazing heroes in this room."

"There was no time for personal desires, there was only the 1 to 2 minutes we all had to make this happen and we did. If any of you, maybe even a single person would have just stood there doing nothing, then maybe we would have ended up with some sort of death and destruction. But everyone did act, and Mattie acted."

"As I stood there waiting to let go after I knew everyone was safe, let go and step back and die...Mattie walked towards me to help me. She was going to pull me from out and under that Ferris wheel to safety. She was crying for me. I haven't had that much in my life and I stopped her with a wave of my hand and by asking her not to endanger herself anymore."

"For the first time in my life, and I have had dozens of days at work that I thought I was going to die and didn't, for the first time ever, and different from all those other times which had me willing to die for strangers, this time I was ready to die for Mattie and your children and for all of you. For if all of you are that important to Mattie, then so are you to me. It was at that moment, I realized for the first time ever I wasn't going to die for strangers but for the woman I love and for her family and friends. Yes you heard me correct. I told Mattie I loved her."

"One of the great things about this country of ours is that fact that no one call tell you who to love or who to hate. The individual gets to choose."

"All those dozens of times that I was on a SWAT call or a 911 call and I thought I might die that day, never was I doing it because I loved that victim or bad guy, it was simply my job and cops die doing their job of serving and protecting. I chose to be a cop to help people and was always prepared to die doing it. I didn't want to die, but was prepared for that eventuality."

"As I stood there in my last few seconds of what I thought was my life I was so proud of Mattie that I asked God as long as she and the others were safe, and at least I got to meet her and kiss her and give her a ride on my motorcycle and watch a sunset with her, I was really ready to die with happiness in my heart because I was finally doing it for the right reasons. For Love. For Mattie."

"My last words before I stepped back and let go of the beam and Ferris wheel collapsed was, softly and while looking into Mattie's crying eyes, the greatest words we can all say to one another, 'I love you.'"

Crowd was crying so a time of silence.

"Of course it wasn't my time, I cheated death again (he must be really pissed at me) and here I am.

Here I am with the greatest group of loving people the earth may have. Here I am with the greatest woman I have ever met. And I ask all of you here tonight, to please take and accept the trauma counseling that will be offered, this trauma can be dealt with and you can all have normal great lives and help each other heal and live with these experiences. Thank you and here is the Doc."

Applause as I walked off the stage.

I walked over to Mattie, who was crying a lot and she hugged me and squeezed me harder than she had ever. I thanked her for everything and people got up from their seats to come over and give us hugs (she let them hug me this time) and everyone was crying and smiling and patting each other on the backs and hugging some more and kisses were flowing freely throughout the auditorium.

Doc yelled out that we would take a 15 minute break before we started back up and Mattie was glowing in her appreciation for my words and from the accolades from the townsfolk.

"Wait until I get you home alone," Mattie whispered to me.

"Good things in my future?" I asked.

"I promise!" She smiled happily.

The meeting started back up and both Docs tried to give me some of the same love that I gave the townsfolk and Mattie and it was nice to hear and I thanked them all for their applause.

Then Doc Snyder began her talk, all about trauma, how counseling can help and after great detail passed around the signup sheet for the townsfolk. Every single one of them signed up for help.

After it was over the hugs and kisses were free flowing again as the townsfolk all went home. The auditorium held only the two docs, Mattie and me and Mattie's parents who were sitting in the back, unbeknownst to Mattie, who now walked up to us.

The two Docs told me and Mattie that they would be contacting us for our personal counseling sessions and begged their pardon, which left just the four of us left. After the parents hugged and squeezed and kissed Mattie half to death, they turned their attention to me.

I shook dad's hand and he came in for a hug. Mom squeezed me so tight, I immediately figured out who taught Mattie to hug, her mom. We all walked back to Mattie's house, talking all the way and both parents were amazed at all the things said in the meeting.

"Everything you said true?" Her dad asked me.

"Absolutely true, sir. Everyone is a hero and especially your daughter."

"But what you did?!" Mom asked.

"I did it for your daughter," I said calmly. "I could not allow harm to her and the people she loves."

Back at Mattie's place, we all ate and ate and ate some more and the tequila helped my constant pain almost as much as the walk did earlier. Her parents excused themselves for the night (they live 3 doors down from Mattie's house) and we were left alone.

Mattie locked the door.

Quite a day huh?" I asked Mattie.

"Come here you!" She exclaimed very quietly, almost in a whisper.

I finally found out what the word, "Ravaged" means. I think she owes me a new t-shirt, pants, socks, underwear and some skin.

Chapter 3
Taking care of Business

This time I was up first and gathering my clothes that were thrown about the house like a tornado. I carefully sat on the bed with a cup of coffee for my sleeping princess.

"Good morning beautiful," I spoke softly to her.

Mattie slowly woke with a most gorgeous smile and said, "Good morning to you!"

She kissed me and took the cup of joe from my hands.

"Good coffee!" She exclaimed and settled in a seated position in her cloud of a bed.

"You are up early."

"I feel great this morning and I have a lot of business to tend to today."

"What kind of business?" She asked.

"Tons of business," I answered.

"Secretive huh?"

"No. I will tell you all about it later," I stated.

"What are your plans for your yellow dress?" I asked her as I looked at it lying over the arm of a chair, all dirty and dusty and not as bright as it once was and unmoved since the night of the incident.

"Why?" She queried.

"I have some plans for it if I can have it," I explained.

A moment of silence then, "I don't think I could ever wear it again, even though I know you love it, so go ahead and take it, it's yours," she said to me.

"Didn't you say you had neglected the retirement home enough and wanted to go in for few hours of work this morning?" I asked.

"Yes, but just for a few, then I want to come back to take care of you," she cooed.

"Well, my business will take about that long, so we may end up finishing at the same time. And I am sure I will be worn out by then and ready for a nap."

I was already dressed and ready to go.

"Before I leave, tell me, does this wonderful town have a lover's lane?" I queried.

"Yes it does, why?" She asked me.

"I would like you to take me there today."

"It's a date!" She said excitedly.

I leaned over and kissed her for what seemed like hours, but it was not enough. I almost reworked my plans for the morning to stay with her.

"I will see you later beautiful and not soon enough," I told her and out the door I went holding her yellow dress in a sack I found in her kitchen.

First order of business that morning was a walk over to the bank. The town only had one and Mattie said it was wonderful. I went in and asked to speak with whoever was in charge and I quickly found myself sitting in an office of the banker himself.

"Nice to meet you Mr. Buchannan, Mattie speaks highly of you and your staff," I advised him.

"Nice to meet the hero in person, it was a brave thing that you did," he stated.

"I'm glad I was there to help everyone save each other," I replied back.

"What can I do for you?" He asked.

"I have a few requests of you and your bank, maybe not your usual ones, but requests nonetheless."

Then I proceeded to lay out my plan of action:

"First, I want to deposit $5,000 into Mattie's bank account.

Next I would like you to make out five different $1,000 cashier's checks and I would like you to disperse them to the five people or families in this town that need it the most. I am talking five people or families that this kind of money will make a big difference, for a short while at least, but a difference. I believe you would know this better than anyone. Tell them it is from an anonymous donor.

Then, I would like another two cashier's checks, in the amount of $1,000 each made out to Doc Sanchez and to Doctor Snyder and I will take those checks with me when I leave here today.

And I trust that this business will be confidential between you and me?"

"Absolutely, give me and my staff a few minutes and you'll be on your way," he stated professionally.

As I waited I walked in the bank's lobby and was looking at the framed pictures on the walls. Black and white photos of early people and the history of this town. I found one that seemed to show Mattie as a baby with her young parent's holding her in front of their house.

Mr. Buchannan called me over to his office and I re-entered and sat down.

"Everything is done and here are your two checks for the doctors. Is there anything else we can do for you?" He asked me.

"Yes, take this for your time and trouble and please buy lunch for your staff one day this week on me and thank you very much," I said as I handed him two $100 bills.

"This is too much," he started to say, but I was already out of his office and out the door of the bank.

I then walked over to Doc Sanchez's office, hoping to find him in. Once there his secretary said he was at the auditorium preparing for their first trauma counseling session.

"Great, I will go over there and thank you," I told her as I walked out through the door.

A minute later I found myself inside the auditorium and it was about 15 minutes until the start of the first trauma counseling session.

Both Docs saw me and waved and before I could get to them to talk, some townsfolk came up to me to shake my hand and tell me they were glad to see me up and around.

Once with the Docs, I asked them for some private time and Doc Snyder asked me, "Are you coming to this session?"

"Not this one, I have some business to take care of right now, but why don't you both plan on coming over this evening for supper at Mattie's place about 6 pm and we could do our first counseling session there," I explained.

"That would be great, we will finish with two sessions by then," they both said at the same time.

"I have something for you both." And I handed them each their check and continued, "Just a little something for patching me up and helping this town, there is more of that if needed."

They both looked dumbfounded.

"Am I offending you?" I asked them.

"No, just very unexpected," they both stated.

"I have a request for you both," I said.

"What is it, anything?" Doc Sanchez said.

I handed them the sack containing Mattie's yellow dress. They looked in and were somewhat surprised.

"I would like to ask you both to get everyone that attends these counseling sessions to autograph this yellow dress with a permanent black marker pen. Men, women, children, all. When it is done, take it over to the hobby shop and they will frame it. I'm going over there next to prepay for it and order a large brass plague to go on the very large glass framed yellow dress when it is done. Also, maybe after all the counseling sessions are done, could you call one last meeting for a town party and we can present this framed dress to Mattie publically?"

They looked at each other and smiled.

"Of course we can do all that," they said together again.

"Secrecy is of the utmost, no one can let her know that this is coming," I pleaded.

"Of course, consider it done."

"Thank you both and see you later tonight."

Next I went over to the hobby store, where they frame pictures and items and told them what I wanted, asked for secrecy and paid them in advance and left.

As I was walking home, I took gauge of myself and decided I felt real good after all these tasks and instead of going home to take a nap and wait for Mattie, I would surprise her and go to the nursing home.

Once there, staff told me where she was and said I was allowed to go in there since I was the hero. I asked the nurse if she was at the fair that day and she said yes and I told her that she was a hero too.

I quietly walked into a lunch room area and immediately saw four older ladies sitting at a table and Mattie was talking to them and tending to any of their needs. It seems they were eating a late breakfast and almost done.

The ladies saw me approach but Mattie did not since she was so busy.

"Vavavoom!" One of the ladies yelled out.

At this Mattie turned around and ran up to me and hugged me and kissed me.

"Way to go girl!" Another lady yelled out.

"Frisky bunch of ladies we have here I see," I said and we all laughed.

Mattie introduced me to all the ladies and I walked around and gave all of them a kiss on the cheek, to which they seemed like melted butter in my hands.

"I'm watching you ladies; keep your hands off my man!" Mattie scolded us quietly and I then realized that this is where she learned that particular skill.

Everyone laughed some more and after a few words of small talk I made a statement, "I am looking for a beautiful lady to take me to Lover's Lane and do some heavy necking, any volunteers?"

All four ladies raised their hands as high as they could.

"Shame on you ladies and on you Scott," Mattie scolded us all quietly.

"I am almost ready to go with you, give me a minute," Mattie told me.

Mattie left and the small talk continued with the four ladies and me and she returned and said, "Sorry ladies, I have to go, I have to take care of my man before I catch him kissing a dog in an alley somewhere!"

And we all busted out laughing.

Once outside, Mattie turned and embraced me, squeezed me tight and kissed me.

"Lover's Lane here we come!" She yelled and this time not quietly.

It was a long beautiful walk to a small park near the edge of town.

The best part of the walk was holding Mattie's hand the entire way. We stopped a few times to hug and kiss and we finally made it there. There was a single park bench on one side and in the middle a covered pavilion and the entire little park had a cement pathway encircling it for strolling by lovebirds. Lots of flowers lined the edges of the park and I decided this was a perfect place to kiss your loved one.

We didn't waste any time and we kissed for what seemed like hours.

Once we were sated, we began the beautiful walk back to her house.

"Did you get all your business done?" She asked me.

"Yes."

"Tell me about it?"

"Sure."

And I proceeded to tell her of my banking business except for the deposit into her account; I wanted to save that for last.

"You really gave the banker $200 in tips and to buy lunch?" She queried.

"That is especially nice to help out five families, I can think of a few that would benefit," she stated.

"Well, next time I will let your choose where the checks go," I told her.

"Okay," she responded quietly.

She was thinking as we continued walking, "That's a lot of money."

"Remember when I said that an individual gets to choose who they love and who they hate?"

"Yes."

"Well, I have a few more simple beliefs. A good snake is one that runs away from you. Money is not a problem unless you don't have any. And most importantly, no one can tell you how to spend your money. Deposit it in the casino slot machines, donate it to charity, or buy lots of comic books and line your walls," I explained.

"I sold my house and all my belongings to become a wanderer. I have a few cherished items in storage, but I live and travel with the VW beetle and motorcycle…so in other words, along with my monthly cop pension check, I have lots of money in the bank. I never have to work again unless I want to for the rest of my life."

"But $1000 each to both Doctors," she asked.

"Do you think they deserve it?"

"Yes I guess so," she explained.

"What do you think about my money ideas?" I asked her.

"Seems right to me, I wouldn't want someone telling me how to spend my money," she answered.

"How do you feel about receiving gifts?" I asked her carefully.

"I don't know, I don't receive too many gifts other than hugs and kisses and food and laughter from people. I don't really need anything, but I guess I'm like most people, it is always nice to get a present from someone, especially from someone you love," she explained in detail.

"Do you love me?" I asked.

She stopped dead in her tracks. This would be the very first time she would say this to me, if in fact she would say it. She looked at me and grabbed me so that she was looking directly into my eyes.

"I do love you Scott, more than you know and I'm going to show you, believe me," and she kissed me for eternity.

When we stopped kissing and began to walk again, I said, "Great, because I put $5,000 in your bank account this morning."

We stopped again.

But before she could say anything, I put my hand upon her lips very gently and said, "My money, my gift to you and you love me."

She looked at me for a moment and kissed and squeezed me and said I tricked her somehow, but she was glad that she finally told me that she loved me.

"What's the money for?" She asked.

"I wanted to give you a gift of some kind. I don't know about your money situation but I do know you have been taking off work to care for me. I just wanted to pay you back a little and show you I care for you."

We reached her house and went in and this time I locked the door and shut the blinds.

Sometime later as we lay in bed, snuggling close, I asked Mattie if tonight would be a good night to have the Docs over to have supper with us, since we had tons of food, and they were doing two counseling sessions today at the auditorium and they would be too tired to make themselves supper, and we could fit in our first private counseling session with them both.

"Sure, I don't see why not," she said to me.

"Good, because they will be here at 6 pm!"

"What?" she exclaimed and she sat up in bed.

"You tricked me again; pretty soon I'm not going to answer your questions anymore," she joked.

"I hope you will always answer my questions, especially when I ask what I can do for you," I countered.

"Wordsmith, that is what you are, a wordsmith," she said laughing and she squeezed me hard.

Just then a knock at the door.

It was the townsfolk bearing food and drink gifts again and this time her parents were with them.

Mattie quickly got dressed and I let everyone in and the hugs and kisses were flying all over the house. I told everyone that this time they didn't need to rush off after 20 minutes if they didn't want to and to stay and truly visit with Mattie and me. It was early afternoon after all and Mattie and I were rested.

Mattie came out and everyone greeted her like the princess she is. She had a smile from ear to ear and was on the receiving end of a thousand hugs and kisses, especially from her proud parents.

Dad walked over to me and gave me a hug and handed me a bottle of his favorite beer and he had one in his hand.

"Sit down with me a moment Scott?" He asked me and we walked over to a loveseat on the other side of the room. I saw Mattie looking inquisitively as we did and I smiled back at her.

"How are you feeling?" He asked me.

"I am feeling better every day, thank you," I answered.

"I want to ask…how are doing for money…do you need any…we can give you some…" he stammered, almost afraid that he was offending me.

"Thank you from the bottom of my heart, but I have plenty," I told him.

He then stated, "Mom and me want to thank you."

"For what?" I asked him.

"We have never seen Mattie so happy, she is a happy kid, but you have made her even happier, we didn't think it was possible."

"I promise you that I will never hurt her in anyway," I explained to him. "Your daughter is special and I am the luckiest man alive as far as I am concerned."

I changed the subject so as to not make it too uncomfortable for dad.

"I was at the bank this morning and saw the picture of you two holding a baby in front of your house, Mattie I presume?"

"Yes, that picture was celebrating our new house with our new baby girl," he happily explained to me.

"It is a beautiful picture, of beautiful people in this beautiful town…wow, lots of beautiful in there, sorry."

And we both broke out laughing and he went to get us another beer.

And so it went for the next couple hours. Everyone was visiting, laughing and joking and a good time was had by all.

"I can't imagine how wonderful Christmas must be around here," I exclaimed to Mattie when she came up to me for a hug and a kiss.

"This much fun on a Tuesday, wow, Christmas must be really awesome!"

Mattie laughed and said, "Yeah it is like this pretty much year round, and you are right--Christmas is wonderful!" And she kissed me again.

After about 2 hours everyone left with the hugs and kisses and laughter.

Mattie and I sat down, this time exhausted and mused that we had two hours before the Docs got here for supper and counseling.

"You locking the door or do you want me to?" I asked excitedly.

"You do it!" Mattie yelled out as she ran for her bedroom, tearing her clothes off as she went along.

Chapter 4
Dinner & Counseling

The house was ready and the Docs showed up a few minutes after 6 pm. We showed them all the food and the four of us began a feast with our smorgasbord of food selections laid out across Mattie's Table.

Small talk was abundant as the food. The Docs were probing Mattie and me to try and figure out how to set the tone for this particular evening.

I was smarter than that, I was experienced in this wordsmithing and I was immune to their probes. I wanted to focus on helping Mattie first and foremost, since I didn't need any help or so I thought.

Doc Snyder asked me a series of several questions rapid fire to get my honest answers without thought and a chance to think them through.

"How are you feeling tonight Scott?" she asked.

"Wonderful," I answered.

"Mentally back to normal?"

"Yes I think so."

"Been eating well?"

"Yes"

"Exercise?"

"Mattie's seen to that," I stated and she kicked me under the table gently.

"How has your sleep been?"

"Could be better, the pain sometimes keeps me up."

"How about those nights when the pain is not the cause?"

"My mind doesn't shut off."

"And what are you thinking about?"

"About Mattie, this town, and how wonderful it all is," I stated calmly.

"About how you don't belong, do you?"

And I stood up from the table. She got me.

Mattie jumped up and grabbed my arm. "What's wrong Scott?" She asked worriedly.

"I looked at both Docs and said, "We don't want to open my can of worms, trust me. This incident can just be added to the thousands of other ones I carry with me, I want to focus on Mattie please."

We sat down and Mattie said, "I do not want to do this if Scott is going to be upset, he has been through enough. Maybe this is too early for us? Maybe we should just visit?"

Doc Snyder said, "I am sorry Scott, I did not want or expect that kind of reaction from you. I can see if and when we talk with you, it will take much more time to delve into."

"And that is what I want to avoid at all costs, it has taken me almost 30 years to get to where I am, there is no hope of saving me, so I, we, need to keep it buried and help Mattie."

"Now you are scaring me," Mattie interjected.

"Mattie, you have know me for a week now, do you see a problem with me?" I asked her.

"Yeah, you are too good to be true," she said as she kissed me.

"Then don't worry about me mentally, I take care of myself," I answered. "I am who you have seen this past week; I am not lying to you or faking it in anyway. I just have to follow a regimen to keep myself this way."

We finished eating and everyone gathered in the living room, bigger space and softer chairs. The Docs asked me and Mattie what they thought the goals of this counseling session should be.

"To help us get through the incident and problems we may have from the experience," Mattie stated.

My turn and I stated matter-of-factly like an arrogant jackball, "You know I am trained and experienced and I know all the things you will say to us tonight and any of times we meet. Most of it does work, the physical activity, the sleeping, the eating well, making lists of chores to keep you focused, the spending time with happy people and loved ones, never sitting alone, never dwelling on the bad thoughts, avoiding excessive alcohol, etc., etc., all of it."

"Scott, there is no need to be hostile towards us," Doc Sanchez said.

"I am sorry, I never mean to be towards anyone," I stated back.

Mattie squeezed my hand; I could tell she wanted us to stop.

"Mattie tell them what you told me about your biggest problem with the incident," I asked her politely.

"I told Scott the other night, I watched him die. Through my tears and my heart ready to explode in pain, I watched him die. The Ferris wheel collapsed, he told me he loved me and then was gone. I have never felt something like that in my life. It was excruciating.

Then 10 seconds later as the dust settled there he was walking towards me and then fell down and I thought he was dead a second time. How much can a heart take?"

"Doc spent many hours with him, I helped and he was just a patient like at work, but this wasn't work, this was my Scott. We had to make sure we saved Scott, and when Doc Sanchez told me he wouldn't need to be transported to a bigger city for hospital care and that he thought he would be unbelievably okay, my heart exploded again. This time with happiness, but my heart was put through the ringer and has only calmed down a little bit since then."

"Scott with all his generosity and caring and love have made it better each and every day, did you know he took me to lover's lane today for some lunchtime smooching? How do you top that? Well he did by holding my hand whenever he could today, entertaining my father and friends and neighbors here for 2 hours before you both got here, and for kissing me thousands of times this week and each time making like it was the very first time he ever kissed me.

I know I will be alright. It gets better every day. With Scott here by my side, with all that he is and does and he teaches me all the time, not by telling me the answer, but by helping me come to the answer on my own. He is smart, kind, loving and now, my friend."

"He takes care of me, in fact the other night he was up all night because of pain and he let me sleep. He told me it was his turn to make sure I got a full restful night of sleep.

He has done other things, secrets I can't share with you, but they are all good."

Both Docs looked at each other and smiled.

"I will be okay, I have no doubt, but please help Scott, please for me," she pleaded.

Both Docs told Mattie she was doing everything correct and healing everyday and they expected no problems for her as a result of the incident, because she was strong and smart herself and because she had me for support also.

They agreed that I could definitely use some type of help, probably not because of the incident but other deep issues. They asked me if I wanted their help.

"Yes, you can try," I answered hesitantly.

"Start tonight?" They asked.

"Give me a 10 minute break and then we can start, and you better hold onto your hats," I exclaimed, "You have no idea what's coming."

Mattie and I got up to stretch our legs and went outside for some fresh air. The Docs were huddled inside making their game plans.

"What are they going to find inside you Scott?" Mattie asked me softly.

"If it comes out, a damaged soul that may not be repairable."

"You know my saying, 'So my slumped soul can sit up straight?'" I asked her quietly.

"Yes."

"That is because my soul can no longer stand up."

And she hugged me for five minutes and we didn't utter another word.

The Docs called us back in and had water for both of us on the coffee table, another key that showed the Docs knew what they were doing.

"You ready to earn your $1000 each?" I quipped. "And that will be the last snotty thing I say tonight, I hope. I'm sorry."

"Let's begin where you want to, start us off Scott," Doc Snyder said softly.

"What's wrong with me? What's wrong with me? Where do I start? I guess by eliminating what's not wrong with me. You heard Mattie describe me, I have heard those descriptors my whole life, so I am good there, although I never assume I am better than anyone and I try not having or showing my ego and I truly care about people or I wouldn't have done what I have in my life."

"I guess what's wrong with me is that I never had what you all have here. In this beautiful little town. I've never had someone like Mattie in my life. I've experienced a woman's kiss and touch, but without love it means nothing. Without support and caring, without holding the hand of someone special, why hold hands at all?

Yet all the time I was risking my life on a daily basis and had nothing to return home to. Emptiness or someone who didn't care. After years and years of this I became a tool. An instrument of doing good deeds and risking my life and trying to help people, but always returning home to no one there to help me. No one to care for me.

You know how many dead body calls I have been to in my career? Over 200. No cop likes to go to murder scene or an accident scene or a car wreck or a dead baby's house. We have to touch the bodies, roll over the bodies, exam them for signs of foul play. Do we arrest the parents or console them?

Then being me, I started volunteering every time a dead body call came over the radio. I figured, that after 40-50 bodies over a few years, that I would save my cop buddies the anguish and I would take them all. 200 dead bodies vs. 40 bodies, surely there is no difference to the effect it would have on me? I was wrong.

I moved away from Arizona for one reason. So I didn't drive down a road and get a memory trigger from a location then remember the dead body call in great detail.

That is one of my problems; I can remember every detail of a 911 call 20 years later. Something has to trigger the memory, but then I have it all. So I watch TV sparingly, read books carefully, avoid some music, anything to not trigger a memory. This isn't for just dead body calls; it is for all 911 calls."

"How does someone help me with this? And still I had no one I could lean on. What was I going to do, go to my parent's house and tell them all about it over dinner? Make them throw up their food? This is not something you can talk to people about, they wouldn't understand, they couldn't help. Mom used to always ask me for funny stories and they were far and few between. It was not in its nature for cop work to be funny."

"Do you know one of my first arrests was a husband beating his wife and one of my last arrests before retirement was his son beating his wife? How am I supposed to deal with that I ask you?"

"So day after day, week after week month and year etc., this stuff added up. No outlet for my soul. I felt it bending over, slouching, and begging me to let it go. Suicide was out of the question but I always searched for the Ferris wheel type incident. Always. And I wanted to live.

I volunteered for every dangerous assignment, even when everyone always said to never volunteer for nothing. I did. I was first to step up always. It became so common place, commanders told me I was not volunteering and that someone else needed to step up and then I doubled my effort to volunteer.

Not suicidal, just, I didn't matter to anyone. I was just this machine disguising himself as a man.

I worked out. My God, a person almost can't work out more than I did. I ate fairly well and didn't drink alcohol and believed in the Bible and joked and laughed with everyone I could. But I went home alone and unplugged myself from the world.

It got so bad after a few years that I trained myself not to think at all during my off time. Not meditating, but an empty, non-thinking mind. Like a machine, a toaster, unplugged from the wall.

Then I retired and I can't do that anymore, so I avoid anything that will trigger a memory of a past 911 call, or a dead body call or a husband beating his wife call, of which I dealt with thousands. I've arrested about 4,000 individuals in my career. I can be triggered to remember every single one of them."

"Since I retired and no longer wear the uniform, now I am a machine with no outlet to help people and I still don't have anyone to help me with the nightmares and the memories. I don't want to be alone or a machine anymore.

And I had all the accolades to prove I was great at my job. Officer of the year awards, of the month, heck one month I actually was awarded detective of the month and I was a patrolman. Never done before, how do you like that?"

"But a commendation or an award doesn't help you sleep at night. It doesn't chase the demons away.

People ask God why he allows suffering. I saw and lived that suffering every single day for 20 years. And couldn't tell anyone about it. Had to keep it inside. How's that?"

"Did you know my academy started with 44 recruits? 20 years later only two of us retired, the rest were gone, some dead, most quit, some fired, others left for other jobs. Two out of 44, I ask you, who were the smart ones out of this group?

And today, a new academy anywhere in the USA doesn't expect a single recruit will make it to retirement. What does that tell you?

Well I stayed and I fought my whole career. Because somebody had to. And I knew I could, I just didn't know it would destroy me along the way. And once I realized I was being destroyed and I had no one to turn to, I became a machine with a 20 year shelf life.

Please understand, that I seemed normal most of the time outwardly and I could easily be the life of the party on demand, or I could be a wallflower and sit there and listen. I was well liked and even loved greatly by my parents and others. My sense of humor was second to none, even beyond weird many times, but made people think."

"I loved helping people. Many would stop me years later in a grocery store, or any public place, remembering my name, giving me a hug or a handshake and telling me that I saved their life or changed their life's outcome permanently to the better. And this is a city of one million people."

"But over the years I saw and felt my soul slipping away. The more it slipped the harder I worked to help people. The more it slouched the harder I tried to stand tall. I searched for anything to help my soul. Prayed to the devil instead of God, that didn't work and was most probably a dumb idea. I read the Bible more, worked out more, ate better, made lists of chores to keep me on track, gave up alcohol, and was never alone."

"I even made a daily ritual, a type of validation for my life. When I went to bed that night I asked myself two questions, "Was anybody glad to see me today?" And "Did I help someone today?" Years later this turned into, "Thank you God for giving me today, but please don't wake me up in the morning." With no hate, or self-pity, I was just done being alone and a machine."

"When I was with my folks or family or friends, I couldn't share, not true sharing, they would never invite me around again if I did. I went places and when asked how my day went I said, 'Fine or okay,' when in fact I held a dead baby that morning, had a friend die that noon, and still had to work a 12 hour shift with wife beaters and stupid human beings."

"It finally got so bad; I sold my house and I now travel looking for peace. I haven't found it yet. 9 years since retirement and I am still searching. 29 years now I have been a machine and no longer want to be. And even though I have searched constantly for my ultimate Ferris wheel incident, I have never found it, so my wandering is either to find peace and love and truly live or finally die saving someone and give me eternal peace."

"Let me tell you three why I went to that Ferris wheel and risked my life and this is the crux of the matter:

I knew all the options in an instant. I knew because I am highly trained and prepared for most of my life for events such as this. I knew what tasks needed to be done. I knew the priority of those tasks. I could help evacuate people from food booths or the fair grounds and only the kids would be injured or killed when the Ferris wheel collapsed. I could have directed traffic out of the east parking lot but again the kids would not have been saved. I could have stood there and did nothing and the whole place would have been full of death and destruction as a result. I could have grabbed three or four guys and we all go and try and brace the 4th leg together, but I knew I could do it alone. And I would never send someone to their possible death, like the dead body 911 call, I will do it for you."

"I knew I couldn't help with the rest but I could brace the Ferris wheel and leave the rest to the others, especially the wonderfully capable Mattie. I watched her for two days and knew if the need arose, I had my field general.

So when the incident came, I calmly (after a beautiful kiss, our last I thought) helped Mattie become the hero she is with my simple directions that she masterfully, with her own abilities, then carried them out to save countless lives.

That is what I do, I plan ahead. I study people, I watch people and I am a trained observer of human actions. Always have, always will prepare for the worst in any given situation and do what needs to be done and save everyone I can, even if I die trying."

"But having said all this, mainly, and this is where it hurts so deep down inside me, this is proof my soul is broken, I became the 4th leg of Ferris wheel, I did it because I am a machine and expendable."

Mattie was crying uncontrollably at this point.

"A worn out, used up 53 year old machine.

I wish I wasn't.

I am not a hero of any sorts, just a machine who will die to save you or help you wherever I can."

"Of course my parents would mourn; they love me and hug me like Mattie's family hugs all the time. But a man needs more than his parent's love and I have never had that.

At the fair, it is either me or a father of three, the same size as me, tough, smart etc. One of us has to go become the fourth leg of the Ferris wheel to save the children. Who do you send? Me or the married father of three?

Exactly, I am expendable."

"Not that anyone wants me to die, I understand that, but my soul doesn't understand this anymore. My soul doesn't want to continue the way I am, and thus my wandering, I'm trying to save myself."

"It doesn't matter all I do if I don't matter to someone else. I am not a machine, I am a man."

"But this time, when I told Mattie that I loved her, that was new. It was from my heart to hers. I had never risked my life with love involved. It was always non-personal. This time my soul and I felt love from Mattie. I saw her crying from the bottom of her heart and soul for me, for me."

"Mattie enabled me to stand tall and have the strength to save the children. Because of her I could have held up two Ferris wheels. Because of her I had no pain when it should have been excruciating. Because of her my body was strong when it should have been crushed and destroyed."

"If Mattie would not have been there, perhaps I would not have had the strength and there would be dead and injured children at the fair."

"In this last week I have been asked how I did what I did. I have told everyone that asked that it was possible because I had the love of a great woman at the very end, supporting and caring for me."

I was silent for a few seconds.

"I have great hope Mattie is the one to make me nonexpendable and turn this machine into a man."

Silence again.

"That my friends, is my can of worms we should have never opened."

Everyone was exhausted.

Silence for awhile.

"You gave us a lot of information to sort through; I think it best if we meet again tomorrow to continue, if that is okay with you both?" Maria said.

Mattie and I looked at each and said at the same time, "Yes."

The Docs left and Mattie was sitting there in a daze.

"Wow you can talk!" She stated.

"I'm sorry," I said quietly.

"No, no, I'm not scolding you I'm just saying," she answered. She crawled closer to me and kissed me and snuggled under my left arm to get closer to me.

"Do you want to talk anymore right now or say anything?" I asked her while rubbing her cheek gently.

"No. I think quiet time would be best for both of us."

"Are we good, you and me?" And at this she jumped up and kissed me and said, "We should be good for another 30 years!" Then she snuggled back under my chin and left arm and my tears started to flow freely.

Chapter 5
Chit Chat

Mattie and I slept without making a stir, her bed of clouds protecting us while we rested peacefully all night long.

We awoke together and I asked, "You getting the coffee or am I?"

"You get it," she whispered.

"Honeymoon's over!" I whispered back as I tried to get out of her bed and she grabbed me and pulled me back in.

"I'll show you a honeymoon mister!" She answered back.

It was awhile before I got up to go make the coffee.

We had no plans for the day as far as I knew, so we got up later than normal, we needed the rest after yesterday's events, and we both were picking through the food for some breakfast snacks.

"Coffee's done sweetheart," I stated softly to her.

"Do you like to be called sweetheart?" I asked her.

"You can call me anything and I will like it," she cooed back.

"Murgatroyd?" I asked.

"Okay, evidently not anything," she said dryly.

"Can I teach you a secret code? We used a thing called 'Empty Hands' in SWAT, basically a sign language so bad guys didn't hear our radios squawking or us talking," I asked her.

"Sure, teach me," she answered.

"I'm going to teach you my very favorite one, so if we can't talk out loud we can still communicate with each other," I responded.

"Hold one finger up for 2 seconds, then add a second finger up for two seconds and then add a third finger. Now hold the three fingers over your heart," I explained.

Mattie did this and looked at me and she asked, "Okay, what does that mean?"

"It means, 1-2-3 I love you."

"And SWAT guys do this between each other?" She exclaimed wildly.

"Of course not, we use other ones with SWAT, I just didn't think you would let me teach you otherwise," I laughed.

Mattie threw a pillow at me from her chair, "You!" She yelled softly.

"Your new training may come in handy someday, you're welcome," I stated warmly.

A knock on the door.

"It's too early for the townsfolk, wonder who it is," I said as I opened the door.

"Come in Doc, want some coffee?" I stated.

"No thanks, not staying, just wanted to ask you both something," he replied.

"What's up?" I asked.

"We are doing our last town wide counseling session today and will be done at 3 pm and Maria and I talked quite a bit last night after our session with you two. We agree that we would like to do it different next time, which could be this afternoon at 3 p. m. if you are amenable to this," he explained.

"We want the four of us to do the session while we are decorating the auditorium for Saturday's party," he stated.

Mattie asked, "What party?"

"The Heroes Party of Hillsboro Fair," he stated excitedly.

"Will it be private enough for us?" I asked.

"The doors will be locked and signs posted for privacy," he answered.

Mattie and I looked at each other, I said, "What do you think Murgatroyd?" And she laughed and said back, "Ok Ichabob, I'm with you!"

The Doc didn't quite know what to make of us and said, "So are you coming?"

"See you at 3:00 pm Doc," she stated.

And he left.

"What would you like to do for the next five hours?" I asked the beautiful woman sitting next to me.

"Hmmmnnn, I don't know," she sighed.

"I think," she mused, "That I kiss you for awhile, then we go get some late breakfast at the diner, then I kiss you some more, then we walk to lover's lane again and really kiss you some more, then I'm not sure, maybe kiss you some more and then it will be 3:00 pm."

"I like your thinking gorgeous!" And the kiss fest began.

We ended up doing all those things and amazingly it was 2:30 pm when we walked back into her house.

We quickly showered together and got dressed and walked over to the auditorium right on time. The counseling session was just getting done and about 30 people were leaving. We got lots of greetings and hugs and kisses as they exited and we entered. Some of the townsfolk were smiling a little too much; I knew something was going on.

"Doing a little more than counseling I take it," I asked both Docs as we walked in.

"How do you know?" Doc Sanchez asked me.

"The wry smiling faces on some the townsfolk as they were leaving, the 'I have a secret that you don't know' look to their faces," I stated.

"You were terrible as a kid with your presents I bet," Doc Snyder stated dryly.

"How long have you two been a couple?" I asked the Docs.

"Scott!" Mattie exclaimed quietly.

"Why do you think we are a couple?" Maria asked.

"Maria, you were willing at the drop of a hat to come to this town and help Doc Sanchez's people. For no pay, without hesitation. You are left handed and the Doc is right handed and when you sat at Mattie's table, you sat on the left and the Doc on the right. Couples would do that, non-couples wouldn't know which hand the other uses to eat or write with. You both have a dry and great sense of humor, usually if only one of the couple has a dry sense of humor and the other does not, it will not work out between them. Seen too much like sarcasm to the other one and not tolerated very well. Doc always holds the door for you, makes sure your seat is ready for you, brings you coffee and food and basically shows that you mean the world to him. I am surprised that you both don't kiss in public, I believe everyone in town knows you both love each other."

Stunned looks from both the Docs.

"Scott, you are incorrigible!" Mattie yelled softly at me.

"Also, the beautiful 11 inch by 14 inch framed picture of you both in Doc's office was a dead giveaway!" I laughed out loud explaining.

"When did you see that?" Doc asked me.

"Yesterday, I went to your office first looking for you and your secretary sent me here to find you. I saw it through your open office door, behind your desk."

"That is a long distance away from the receptionist's counter," Doc mused.

"I have great vision and notice things," I stated in response.

"I did not mean to offend you both," I said apologetically.

They looked at each other and he said, "We are just not as open and rambunctious as you too are, jealous actually, and we talked about that last night after spending time with you both. Can we walk with you to lover's lane next time you go? We believe you two could teach us a lot," he asked sheepishly.

"Hahahaha! Absolutely you can, but just who is going to be kissing who?" I asked loudly and with great joy.

"Scott!" Mattie yelled at me, this time a little louder.

"You are always welcome to join us!" Mattie said. "And we would love to have you over at my house anytime," she added.

Then Doc Snyder (Maria) turned serious in her demeanor.

"We hope that no matter how the counseling goes, you two will still be our friends?" She stated. "You are not just clients to us," she added.

"Are you expecting bad results?" Mattie asked quickly.

"You never know the results you will get," Maria stated quietly.

"Friends first, clients second," I stated. And everyone agreed.

We began with multiple tables with various decorations for the auditorium. Large ones, small ones and both Docs stated we would decorate only until the counseling session was over then tomorrow a bunch of townsfolk would come in the morning to finish up. The purpose of this type of session was to get away from sitting and looking at each other and make us do two things at once: decorate and talk.

"Can we have smooch breaks?" I asked quietly. Mattie smiled. Doc Sanchez yelled out, "You bet!" Which shocked Maria a little bit. We all laughed.

"Scott, today's session will be more question and answer, we are not expecting a repeat of last night, it may take us years to decode everything you said," Maria said dryly, but in a nice way.

"We are looking, not to trick you in any way, but to get the very first answer that comes to both your minds, that is where we learn the most of your minds and if we can help you," she added.

"If you can help us?" Mattie queried.

"Not everything cannot be fixed," Maria answered.

Mattie frowned and I grabbed her hand in mine and kissed her on her cheek.

Maria started the session, "Mattie will be okay with this incident. Scott, we don't think it bothers you, but it is another in that collection of yours of bad experiences. Your collective of demons is your problem and we have no doubt you can help Mattie with any issues that might arise for her, and we believe that Mattie can help many of your issues too.

But let me do a small narrative for you both before we start the Q & A session. We looked up a lot of stuff last night from Mark's office. We could find no information or sketchy information at best in regards to cop problems like Scott described last night. We could find war related studies from soldiers and their problems upon returning home but that is radically different in so many ways from what Scott endures. Their war may be a year only or more, but Scott's war was 20 years."

"So Mark and I decided to go back to basics and ask questions based on reality vs. dreams, consequences of failure, expectations, aspirations and words of wisdom."

"We do not know how much if any help we can provide Scott, we are fighting against 29 years of fortifying his psyche. And it may not let us in to help. But if that is the case, we have lots to offer to make his life better, even little bits here and there will be better than what he has now. And this does not have to be the last session; we can talk and work together for as long as necessary."

"Smooch break!" I yelled and Mattie slapped me as she came in for some serious kissing. Doc and Doc smooched too. And we all laughed when we were done.

"Scott, what do you want?" Maria asked me.

"Peace and love," I answered.

"What is peace to you?"

"Holding hands, being loved, being needed, and being valued."

"Valued as what?"

"A real person, who I am."

"What happens if that person that values you, scolds you, how would that make you feel?"

"I would try my hardest to not do whatever I did to make them mad at me."

"For fear of losing them?"

"No, out of respect."

"What is love to you?"

"Mattie."

"Explain."

"I can't in a short, simple answer."

"Try."

"If you told me I could only have one thing out of this list from Mattie today: sex, hold hands, hugs, or talk, I would choose hold hands."

"Why?"

"They lead directly to her heart and soul."

"I don't understand?"

"Talk is great, awesome, I love talking to her. Hugs from Mattie are to kill for, let me tell you and they warm me up from the inside out. Sex, she is the sexist woman in the world! Holding her hands, there is love in her hands. She has helped deliver babies into this world, wiped the faces of elderly women in the old folks home when they have food on their chin, served food to family and friends and strangers with her hands, and they hold me when she hugs me, do all sorts of things when we have sex and she now knows how to talk with them in secret SWAT hand code. So I would take the hands today."

Both Docs looked over at Mattie who was smiling tremendously.

"Well," Maria said, "What's the SWAT hand code?"

Mattie showed them three times, they followed her and practiced and then they asked her what it meant.

"1-2-3 I love you," she told them.

"That's not cop code!" Mark yelled out.

"No, but it's the best code you could ever learn," Mattie said with conviction.

"Smooch break!" Mark yelled and we were all at it again.

We decorated, we talked, we decorated and we talked. It actually was a very fun afternoon full of insights for all four of us. We learned about Maria and Mark, some things Mattie didn't even know. But the seriousness of the meeting had to come back.

"What do you want from Mattie?"

"Whatever she will give me."

"Be more specific."

"I hope she likes me for who I am, flawed and all. I hope she will see my good points, most importantly, I hope she values me and makes me nonexpendable."

"What does nonexpendable mean here?"

"It means, that I have value, some value, enough to make Mattie want to be with me, kiss me, walk with me, eat with me and not just for this week or next, but for a long time to come," I stated.

"Forever?"

"If I am lucky enough."

"What if she doesn't want you forever?"

"Then I will graciously accept whatever she will give me and for as long as she will."

"Wait a minute!" Mattie butted in.

"There's a reason for these types of questions Mattie, bear with me please," Maria said to her.

"What if this is a disaster stress type of romance and it doesn't last?"

"I fell in love with her two days before the incident."

"When and how?"

"The very first time I met her; she walked up to me in the diner and asked what I wanted from her. I told her I wanted to see if her eyes matched the rest of her and she laughed. That was it for me. Next was later that day, I looked up, all sweaty and dirty from helping the men folk set up the fair and it was the first time Mattie did not roll her eyes at me but smiled. That was two. Finally, later that night when she wanted my dirty clothes to wash and she wouldn't avert her eyes or walk away and I had to strip naked in front of her to give her all my dirty clothes and she laughed at my red underwear. If you can't fall in love after those things, you are hopeless."

Mattie was shaking her head and laughing, as she continued putting up decorations, having never turned around to face us while I was answering that question.

"Do you know Mattie's full name?"

Mattie turned around at this question to see how I was going to answer.

"Matalena Elizabeth 'Mattie' Haynes. 40 years old, born March 12, 1977.

Parents Charles D. Haynes and Mother Elizabeth Maria Gonzalez.

Local high school, state university, degree in Nursing. Works for Doc Sanchez and donates her time at the nursing home with all those crazy, out of control ladies.

Bought her own house with her own money. Strong willed, amazing kisser. Likes French toast.

Beloved individual of the town of Hillsboro and I imagine surrounding areas."

Silence for awhile. Stunned looks on all three faces.

"Your father told me the other night as we were drinking beers, he is a cool old man for sure!" I shouted out to all three.

And everybody laughed.

"I get the sense you three are just waiting to be amazed by me, am I wrong?"

"Well…"

"Yeah I guess…"

"You already amaze me Scott," Mattie said quietly as she came in for a, "Smooch break!" She yelled.

"You told us last night that you couldn't tell anyone of your collective. Do you want to tell Mattie?"

"I would never tell her."

"Why?"

"It would hurt her."

"Then how does she help you with them?"

"She holds my hand; she hugs me if they appear."

"Then you will tell her of them?"

"No, I would never tell her under any circumstances."

"We don't understand how she will help you?"

"You have felt love in your life haven't you Doc? And a bad thing happened and that person helped you through it correct?"

Doc said, "Yes."

"I had a single problem and had no one. Then I had dozens of issues. Later hundreds of bad experiences happened to me and then thousands. Never was there someone to hold my hand, hug me, and tell me everything would be okay. Imagine if Mattie had been there all those years to do those things for me, do you think I would be the same as I am now, or a happier, better human being?"

"You get a cut on your hand. Could a person help prevent it from happening in the first place? Make it heal immediately? No. But they can console you, hold you, kiss you and bandage you up. I never had that during my career."

"A cut on the hand, you would tell her how you acquired it. Damage to the soul you keep to yourself. The things I saw and did stay with me only. They are not to be shared with others, ever.

Mattie will be there for me so I am not alone. She will tell me everything will be okay. She will bandage me up and help me heal. And sooner than later you don't even feel the cut anymore. But you feel the kiss, the hug, the touch and the care given by another human being."

"Do you have a high tolerance to pain?"

"Short term, I can block pain."

"Nerve damage?"

"No."

"Why don't you feel pain?"

"I block it mentally, I handle it and I shut it down, I don't want to be distracted by it."

"Give me an example?"

"House/garage fire, I went in, removed people, dog, cats, large items that were on fire. Drove engulfed car out of garage into open air away from the house. Saved house from burning down. Firemen, ambulance crew arrive 20 minutes later and finish the job. They noticed my right hand and arm and back. 2nd degree burns, permanent scarring…I didn't even notice. Went to ER, they searched my nose and throat, deep exams, extremely fast."

"Why?" Mattie asked.

"Looking for scorching in my throat and burnt hair inside my noise, if I had those from breathing in hot air or flames…"

"You would have been dead within an hour," Mark stated softly.

"But my nose was clear; throat clear, docs in ER couldn't understand it. The t-shirt I was wearing was melted to my chest. My beard and hair were burned off."

"I held my breath every time I went into the burning garage, about a dozen times or so," I said calmly. 'I told the ER Docs that it was prudent to do so.' And they looked at me funny."

"ER docs couldn't understand why I was not screaming in pain from the 2nd degree burns on right hand and arm up to my shoulder. They pulled melted pieces of debris out of my back. 'I asked the Docs if I they wanted me to scream?' 'No,' they said, 'but you should be.'"

"Next, another nurse came in with a sandpaper looking glove on. They told me he would scrape off all the burnt and dead skin and that he would rake my hands and wrist and forearm and elbow and it would really hurt, 9 on 10 pain scale. He said they would put silver cream on the wounds immediately after and it would take most pain away and help healing. They asked if I was ready and the male nurse scraped my hand until it was bleeding all over the bed and table. Skin was coming off like crazy. I just sat there." 'Why aren't you screaming?' 'Because I can take this pain,' I told him."

"No one knew what I carried inside me all the time, this was nothing. I could shut off or turn on whatever I wanted to with my mind and body."

"The Fire Chief and police, hospital staff and family members all asked me why I went back again and again inside the burning structure. And I told them I knew I could do it; I knew I could save the house."

"I can cut off pain, I can't stop from passing out from pain, 10 on a 10 scale, but I can handle a 9 better than most. I can go without sleep for as long as needed or sleep for 24 hours straight. I can slow down my heart rate, my breathing. I can have sex as long as a woman wants, a few minutes or a few hours, I can control it," they looked at Mattie and she nodded yes.

"I can lift weights that men my size couldn't. Perhaps these are results of making myself a machine, an unplugged toaster, freeing my mind of thinking, which I did for so many years, that is my best guess."

"And don't assume I feel no pain, I can just handle the pain."

"Did you feel pain with the Ferris wheel?"

"No."

"Why not? Surely you felt you ribs cracking, your back breaking, your shoulder and sternum being crushed? You heard Mark say you should have died?"

"I felt none of those things."

"But how?"

"I told you I could have held up two Ferris wheels."

"How could you do that?"

"With the strength Mattie gave me and my soul."

"We do not understand."

"Always try to understand the big picture. I only had to do this task for a minute or two. Not an hour, a day or week. One or two minutes."

"I can, any human, is capable of doing most anything for that time period. If I would have succumbed to pain, I would not have been able to help Mattie and the others to save the children and the others. I would not have been able to watch Mattie in action. My mind would have been cloudy; I wanted to be clear to watch her be a hero."

"Why was that important to you?"

"Because it was going to be the last thing I ever witnessed."

Mattie was crying now, and hugging me hard. I kissed her softly and kept my mouth on her cheek.

"But why think of someone else in your last seconds of life and not yourself?"

"I am not on the same level as everyone here. Mattie and the rest are above me, nonexpendable, they have everything a human could want, and then lower down, substandard life was where I live. Toaster world. They deserved to live. I didn't want to die, but I had to, or Mattie or a child she knew or her neighbors might have died.

But it wasn't my call to say if I lived or not, that goes to a higher source. But I did have say in who was going to live that evening. I had that power and I used it to the best of my abilities."

"Tell me about this power you have."

"I know all three of you have seen dead bodies because of your professions. Do you agree that the life spark, the soul or whatever you want to call it is gone from the body once it's dead?"

All three nodded their heads up and down.

"That soul is all powerful, whether or not a person uses that strength. It fuels us, makes us alive and when it is time it leaves our husk behind and goes somewhere. I believe to heaven or hell. But it goes somewhere.

Maybe you don't feel your soul when it is healthy, stands tall and guides you, talks to you while you are asleep.

Most people take their bodies, feet, hands, etc., for granted. But twist your ankle, sprain your wrist and they become whiners and complainers until they get healthy again and then they forget about their ankles and wrists like before. Take it for granted until it hurts."

"I know that a soul can be hurt and be crippled. I have one. It is constantly fighting to be healthy like our bodies do, but too much damage can stop it from happening. Cut off a leg, the body can't grow another one. But your unhealthy soul talks to you all the time. It never shuts up. It questions your choices; maybe some of them have caused the damage to your soul, perhaps others not. It asks and sometimes demands to leave your body. It doesn't want to be broken and injured and crippled up. Weigh your soul down too much, it can't stand up."

"This power, are you talking adrenalin?"

"No. I'm talking about the soul. Adrenalin never came into play here."

"How is that possible?"

"I am sure most people at the fair had adrenalin rushes, the fight or flight syndrome stuff, but I didn't and neither did Mattie."

"How do you know that about Mattie?"

"I watched her the whole time."

"Adrenalin is the enemy of the cop or fireman, or fighter or military person. We cannot have adrenalin dumps/rushes or we are ruined. Understand an Olympic level athlete with an adrenalin rush will be superman for 40 seconds. A typical house wife or beer gut male citizen might be a superman for 10-15 seconds. They all have the same thing in common. With adrenalin rushes you only get one. So after your time is up, you want to go sleep somewhere. You do not have the strength to run to save your life anymore; you fall over and go to sleep. Your body pays a price to be superman for a few seconds, if you didn't get away or stop the bad guy, then you may die.

It should be called an 'escape quickly once or die' dump to be more accurate on its usage."

"So you had no adrenalin that night?"

"Of course not, or I would have failed, I have trained most my life to not get an adrenalin rush. That's what military, police, medics and others train for, to do our jobs under stress without adrenalin.

"I held the Ferris wheel from collapsing for 2 minutes, not 40 seconds. If I had adrenalin in me then the Ferris wheel would have collapsed at the 30-35 second mark, because I am surely not an Olympic level athlete."

"And I would not have witnessed Mattie in action."

"You come back to that a lot, why is that so important to you?"

"All that she shared with me the previous few days and the fact that she wore that yellow dress for me, for me. Mattie made my soul stand up and it has been years since that last happened, it was something I thought not possible ever again for me after so many years of trying."

"Did you try to lift the Ferris wheel?"

"I didn't have to, I had to keep the Ferris wheel from falling down, and that is all, for 1-2 minutes. Very simple and I got to watch Mattie save lives. Without coordination, without a field general to direct people under stress, if not for Mattie and what she did that day, there would have been dead people at that fair."

"What about what you did that day?"

"What about it?"

"Did you save lives that day?"

"I gave Mattie time to save the others and the others to save everyone else.

"You are dodging the question it seems?"

"A hero has something to lose, I had nothing."

"If I died I gained peace for eternity, which would have been a grand prize for me would it not? But only if I saved Mattie and helped her save the others first. So I did what I did until everyone was out of danger.

If Mattie would have died, I bet thousands of people would have come for her funeral; her parents would never recover from the devastation of her passing. This town would mourn for years at her loss. You know why? Because she is beloved beyond compare, she is nonexpendable in anybody's world. Hers would have been a loss for the entire community. And a life like that is worth saving and protecting."

"Describe Mattie to us and what you want in a woman."

"Mattie is without compare. She is everything I want in a woman. Brave, smart, independent, strong, beyond gorgeous and beautiful, sexy, great outgoing personality, loves to hug and kiss, full of life, generous, kind, caring, supportive, great sense of humor, never afraid to cry, emotionally strong, a genius, loves to go to lover's lane; she is my dream lady."

"You know I think I have seen her get hugged and give hugs about 8,000 times since I met her. A new world record I would say and she says it is normal in this wonderful town. I thought my mom was the best hugger in the world; she has some competition from her for sure."

"Where do you see the two of you in 1 year? 5 years? 10 years and beyond?"

"If I am the luckiest man alive and ever born, all those years will see me and Mattie walking to lover's lane, holding hands the entire way and smooching like we just met."

"Do you ever see yourself being on Mattie's and our nonexpendable levels?"

"With her in my life, yes."

The Docs called the session over. They wanted a 10 minute break and Mattie and I turned it into a smooch break. She was still wiping some tears away, when I grabbed her hand to kiss it.

"You okay?" I asked her.

"Yes, I love you," she calmly said to me, "You are something special."

The Docs returned and we all sat around, having stopped the decorating, not that I did much anyway. It was mostly Mattie and Mark, Maria and I were busy talking.

"Well, Mark and I have good news and bad news, which do you want first."

"Bad news."

"Scott, we will keep researching, but this is unchartered territory for psychologists as far as we can tell. There is not much we can tell you to do to 'Save your soul' as you put it. It is beyond our skill level at this time. But hope is not lost."

"Now for the good news:

We believe that alone you are susceptible to problems, with Mattie you are not. We concur with you that if you had Mattie or someone like her all those years you would not be where you are now or have been. Life would have been better for you in so many ways. Support and caring can't heal the cut, but they heal the soul, you are correct. A hug or kiss at the right time could cure your mental aliment that day. Tons of hugs and kisses over time may work wonders. In fact, we think your soul may take up cartwheels to celebrate if you get enough caring and loving."

"We think you have a lot of insight into the soul, most of which we never heard of or thought of and you explained it quite well. We will conduct more research to seek out answers on this topic."

"The collective of demons you carry inside you is a finite number. We don't know what that number is, but since you are retired now and not adding to the collective anymore (except this Ferris wheel incident) time is on your side."

"The more time that passes, maybe hundreds or even thousands of your lesser demons will fade away, leaving fewer demons in number and maybe your soul can deal with them better to make them disappear too, especially with all the good stuff Mattie is giving to you each day feeding your soul."

"Between Mattie and your soul, maybe someday soon, you will be a better than you are now inside, but we all agree, that it would be hard to make you better man on the outside. From what we see and hear, you are a great man."

"And you would be missed beyond compare if we didn't have you here with us, Mattie can attest to that, but so can we and many others that owe their lives to you, hero or not."

"We hope and pray for you and Mattie. We wish you a lifetime of love and happiness and to that end, smooch break!" Maria yelled, much to Mark's surprise.

And the kissing went on and on and on.

Chapter 6
The Party

I awoke to a gorgeous naked lady sitting on top of me.

"Good morning sunshine!" she exclaimed.

"Good morning to you beautiful!" I exclaimed back.

"I guess coffee is going to wait?" I said laughingly.

"It might be time for tequila before we are done!" She said softly and that was the beginning of that.

Sometime later we both got out of Mattie's bed very reluctantly, and even for a second, we thought to just stay there all day, but reality snuck in.

"Big day today, we need to get started," she said.

"I reluctantly concur with your sound judgment," I stated.

"What's with you?" she quipped.

"Just want to sound smart," I said.

"You are smart lover boy, you got me didn't you?"

"Yes, I did, I guess that makes me a genius," I said as I kissed her softly.

I was really beginning to love Mattie's kitchen and coffee table. It always seemed to have plenty of food and snacks on it and was inviting to everyone who sat there.

"I have a few more errands to run this morning, only take about an hour, and then can we talk a walk to lover's lane?" I asked Mattie.

"Of course, I would love to, I will be ready and waiting by the time you get back," she replied.

And with a kiss I was out the door. I quickly headed over to the hobby shop to see the finished product, Mattie's yellow dress, all signed and framed behind glass. Once there I was amazed at how beautiful it looked, about 5 feet tall, 2 foot wide, with the most beautiful wood frame and on a heavy duty ornate metal stand. The bottom of the picture was about 6 inches off the floor; it was so easy to look at for anyone who stood in front of it. The large brass plaque on it looked great and said all the words I wanted it to.

"You did a very wonderful job with this project, I told the store staff. Thank you so very much," with appreciation I said to them.

They said it would be delivered before the 2 pm start of the Heroes Party at the auditorium today and after I laid out two $100 bills in tips on their counter as my thanks, I was out the door.

Next I was off to Mark's office and Maria let me into the locked business/residence. She spent the night with her man it seemed and had the hair and smile to prove it.

"Coffee?" She asked me.

"Sure, I will take a cup," I responded.

Mark came out of the back bedroom and said good morning and sat down with us for a cup of morning joe.

"Everything all set? Is there anything I can do to help?" I asked them both.

They looked at each and said, "Nope, we think we have everything in hand."

"Great! And thank you both for doing all this for me," I stated.

"You are welcome, our pleasure," Maria responded.

"Hey, I'm going to pick up Mattie and we are taking a walk to lover's lane, care to join us?"

"Absolutely. Let's get dressed!" Maria yelled to Mark as she ran to the bedroom.

"Meet us at Mattie's house," I said and I was out the door.

As I walked back, early as it was, I noticed a lot of people in the town. About half the street's parking spots were filled with cars, and I could see that the diner was half full of customers already. Must be here for the party I mused.

Back at Mattie's house, she met me at the door and kissed me for eternity.

"Now that's a greeting!" I told her softly.

"Mark & Maria are going to join us for our walk."

"Great!" And just then they walked up to the open front door.

Pleasantries were exchanged and hugs too and off we went. As we hit the sidewalk and were walking, a couple asked where we were going and Mattie told them. "Can we join you?" They asked. "Sure!" Mattie responded and our twosome became a threesome. As we continued it happened again and again until our group became about 20 or more.

At first I thought we looked silly walking down the sidewalk, such a large group holding our loved one's hands, and then more people left their porches and joined us. By the time we got to lover's lane, we were about 50 couples strong and moved into the middle of the street to continue our walking. All age groups were represented at this park. Once there, Mark yelled out, "Smooch time!" and the festiveness, amongst a lot of laughter, began.

After awhile, the four of us started our leisurely walk back to Mattie's place. The group joined us and split off as we got to their respective places. By the time we reached Mattie's house it was just the four of us.

"We've got to go, lots to do!" Maria told us and after a hug and kiss to Mattie and a handshake from Mark they were gone.

"I've got a present for you," I said softly.

"I already got a few presents from you this morning," she said smiling, "You have more for me?"

"Today, I have a lots of presents for you!" I exclaimed.

And I grabbed two dozen red roses from under a blanket on the front porch. I hid them there before I opened the door when I came back from my errands this morning.

"They are beautiful Scott! Thank you!" As she hugged me with one arm while holding the flowers in the other and kissed my cheek.

"Let's go put them in water," I said.

"They can wait but I can't," she said as she pulled me inside and locked the door.

This time, after, we both stayed in bed and fell asleep. It was about 2 hours later that we stirred.

"What time is it?

"Noon," I replied.

"We better get up and take a shower and start to get ready," she added.

"I concur madam," I stated.

"Weirdo!" she replied lovingly back to me.

As I was washing her back in the shower, she turned around and looked me in the eyes and said, "Thank you Scott for the best week of my entire life!" And she kissed me softly.

"I can do this forever for you if you want me to," I told her softly back.

"I'll take whatever you will give me and for as long as you will," she said and squeezed me hard.

We took our time with our shower, enjoying each other's embrace and the cool water falling down on us like rain.

Refreshed we got dressed and Mattie noticed my usual white v-neck t-shirt was not being put on. And instead of blue jeans I was now wearing black slacks that I pressed earlier.

"No clean shirt? I can go wash one quick," she said excitedly.

"No t-shirt for the party. This calls for a nice button up short sleeve shirt and of course it is pure white, I don't think anyone but you will notice," I said.

She walked over to look at me as I was finishing buttoning it up.

"Oh, they will notice, trust me!" she exclaimed.

"What should I wear?" She asked me.

"The brightest, happiest red dress you own!" I exclaimed.

She went into her closet and pulled out a most beautiful candy apple red dress. It was same style as her yellow one and once I saw it I yelled out, "That's it! It's gorgeous!"

As we walked over to the auditorium, we noticed that there was not a free parking space anywhere to be seen in town. There were many dozens of people milling about on both sides of the street and everyone seemed happy and full of life.

Many people waved at us and we waved back and as we approached the door of the auditorium, we were flooded with handshakes and hugs, many from people I had never seen before. Once inside, this flood of people continued on for about 10 minutes. They were telling us both 'Thank you' and 'Nice to meet the heroes' and such stuff as that. They were really telling us thank you for saving their loved ones life at the fair. I tried to say everyone there was a hero, but I was constantly drowned out by the next person thanking me and Mattie.

"Just go with it Scott and be gracious," Mattie told me quietly, as she smiled deeply into my eyes.

Mattie was absolutely stunning and was most probably hugged by over 100 people that day.

"Save some hugging for me later, would ya?" I joked.

"I save the good stuff for you!" She exclaimed wryly.

Evidently, the shock and potential loss of life of the towns people spread to their families and friends all over and they made the pilgrimage to come see them and offer their support and friendship and to show them they loved them and now today, to celebrate this fact.

We finally made it over to the Docs and Maria was stunning in her own right, "Wow, you are absolutely beautiful Maria!" I gushed. Mark was as happy as a lark standing hand in hand with her.

"You look great too Mark, if I was a woman I'd go for you for sure too!"

"Scott!" Mattie said as she slapped me very softly.

"Do you want to start off Scott?" Maria asked me.

"Yes, I will be ready in one minute, let me go run an errand," I said, and kissed Mattie and walked away.

"What's he up to know?" Mark said.

"No idea," stated Mattie, "We'll see soon enough."

I searched and found the man I was looking for, the banker.

"Good afternoon Mr. Buchannan, how are you this lovely day?" I asked him.

"Wonderful thank you, did you know my daughter was at the fair with my grandson?" he asked me.

"No, I didn't, then they are heroes too and you must be proud of them," I stated sincerely.

He smiled and took out some sealed envelopes out of his jacket pocket and handed them to me.

"Thank you for being such a wonderful banker, Mr. Buchannan," I said politely.

"Thank you for saving my daughter and grandson," he replied back.

I then walked up on the stage and motioned for the crew to bring over the framed dress and set it up, but of course it had a large silk sheet over it to hide what was underneath. Mattie was not to see it just yet.

She started to walk over to the stage, but I motioned her to stay where she was. I walked up to the front of the stage and began:

"Greetings to you all! My name is Scott and I want to say thank you to all the friends and family members who are here today, some of you traveled from foreign countries, back to Hillsboro to give your loved one your love and support. By now, you all have heard every story, every angle of the incident that we all lived through. There are always many facets of such an event, but only one that has any true value—that we all survived. Broken stuff can be replaced, but a human being cannot.

Everyone in this auditorium, whether you were there at the fair the night of the incident, or you supported your loved one in the following days when they came home to tell you of their experience, you are all heroes to me."

"From the bottom of my heart I want to thank all of you that have offered me support this week in the form of food, and drink, hugs and handshakes and the many kind words."

"Could I have Mattie and the Docs up on stage with me?" They all walked up and Mattie kissed me again.

"In this envelope I have a check for $10,000 to become the First Annual Hillsboro Women's College Scholarship Fund. I request it go to a talented, wonderful, brave and intelligent young lady of Hillsboro each year to help with her university degree. Mattie and Maria will be the ones to administer the scholarship.

You may ask why a young lady and I tell you it is because with women such as Mattie and Maria in this town, and we see how amazing they are, I want to ensure more like them for generations to come."

Clapping from the audience.

"In this envelope is $25,000 to both the Docs."

They looked stunned.

"These monies are to help build up your office to double the capacity since I believe we all will be welcoming out newest permanent resident Doctor Maria Snyder!" I stated loudly.

Clapping from the crowd.

"How did he know?" Maria asked Mark quietly.

"I didn't say anything," he answered.

"This town will go from one excellent doctor to two excellent doctors and I want to help this transition go as smooth as possible. And who knows, I may need more stitches someday and we'll see if Maria's handiwork is better than Mark's," and the crowd laughed.

Mark and Maria walked over for their check and they hugged me at the same time.

Mattie was crying all this time and holding her hands to her cheeks.

"And now for the woman I love. I am sure most of you know what I think of her, how proud I am at how she handled herself at the fair and that I believe her to be a hero and that she helped save everyone's lives, including my own.

But how to tell her this with more meaning? First it must be publically. It must be before everyone and for everyone to see now and forever. However, it must not be from just me, but from everyone, from everyone that is grateful beyond words, grateful from the bottom of their heart and soul, grateful to Mattie for the lives saved."

"Mattie, step over here please," I asked gently with my arms raised and grabbed her to hug her and kiss her when she got next to the covered picture frame.

"Survivors of the fair made something for you my dear, they signed it with love from their happy hearts, and the brass plaque reads:

To Matalena Elizabeth Haynes
'Mattie'
Thank you for preventing our broken hearts.
Thank you for giving us life at the risk of your own.
Always remember, you are beloved beyond compare."

And I took off the silk sheet to expose her yellow dress, still dirty and dusty but this time autographed by over 100 people who were at the fair that evening and saved by Mattie. The glass shown as bright as her smile, the wood frame was exquisite.

She walked up to it, touched the glass and read a few names and broke down crying. I quickly grabbed her and held her and whispered in her ear, "I love you."

I looked over at Mark and Maria and they took the hint and yelled out, "Everyone! Help yourself to cake, food and drink, enjoy!"

After all the presentations were made, it seemed like everyone was exhausted but invigorated all at the same time. Everyone was either sitting down or standing up, milling about, eating cake and other sweets or real food and seemed happy. This went on for about 30 minutes, when everyone was sated with food and drink Mattie asked me go outside to do some "Smooch Time" with her. Being the kind minded man I am I would never let a lady such as her down, so I walked outside with her, hand in hand.

"You are amazi..." she kissed me before I could finish.

"No need for talking right now, I need to kiss you more," she cooed and continued.

We kissed for eternity. Or at least 10 minutes, until someone rudely interrupted us and called us back inside the auditorium.

"Who was that lady?" Having not turned around to see who called us. "I'm taking my cake back," I said quietly under my breath.

"It was Maria and no you are not!" she slapped me softly and scolded me the same.

Mattie led the way as we walked back inside the auditorium. I noticed immediately that over 300 people were now standing in the middle of the auditorium floor near and facing the stage. As Mattie walked me up the stairs and onto the stage, I saw the 4 older ladies in their wheel chairs parked up front, but to one side. I saw more elderly people up front to the other side, leaving the middle of the front row for her mom and dad and Mark and Maria and space for Mattie.

Mattie took us to the very middle of the stage, where a big 'X' was taped on the wooden floor.

We stood facing this huge crowd of townsfolk and their folks and families from out of town, out of state and even a few from out of country, who all made the trip here to Hillsboro for this party.

Mattie turned to me and said, "Your talking is over, now it's my turn."

"Hello to you all and thank you for coming here today to celebrate survival and life and each other."

"Everything this week that could be said has been said. Everyone is getting all the help they need to overcome any issues that they have or that might arise from having been involved in the incident one way or another."

"We have heard many speakers and many speeches and counseling sessions this week and we have laughed and we have cried. We are lucky though, because we have each other. We have all the support any person could ever want or need. We do not have to deal with this alone, ever."

"However, I know one person here that has had to deal with hundreds of such events such as this one, and many worse, and never had anyone but himself to lean on. I do not understand how he fought through it all for decades and still became the man he is today. A strong man, a wise man, a generous man, a wonderful man, a loving man, a tender man, my man."

"Scott is quick to praise others, heap glory on them and lend a word of encouragement. He teaches others of great life lessons he has witnessed, to spare them the pain of making the mistake to learn from it.

He gives his money away to others that he thinks need it more than him, or to help make their lives better. He has fame from two decades of his work as a police officer, of which he cares not. He says personal glory is not why he helps people and we all saw that in action one week ago."

"Scott wants to learn how to forget his past horrors he carries inside of him, from those 20 years of seeing humans at their worst and wants to replace it all with peace and love. That searching is what brought Scott to our town. An accidental diversion? The Hand of God? Or whatever drove him into our town, I for one am thankful.

Imagine the fair without him there. Take a look to your right, now to your left, imagine who may not be standing here today. Imagine many funerals all this week and today and even more hospital visits for the injured. Now, Thank God for sending Scott to us."

"Scott asks nothing of us in Hillsboro. He gives and gives and asks for nothing in return. I have never met a man like him and I plan on keeping him for the rest of my life.

Scott longs only to hold my hand, kiss my lips and look me in the eyes and tell me he loves me. To Scott I will give all my kisses until I can't kiss anymore. I will give him all my hugs until my arms are too weak to hold him, and I will give him all of me until I am gone from this earth. That is what I am going to give him, to the man I love."

I was crying pretty hard by now.

"And they also have something to give to you Scott," she said as she walked past me off the stage and motioned for me to stay there.

Once she was in the front row, being hugged by her mom and dad, she raised her right hand as high as she could. The crowd mimicked her action. She held out one finger, the crowd followed. She then added a second finger to the first and the crowd followed. And then a third finger and the crowd followed again. They held their hands high for a few seconds and then everyone touched their hearts.

I lost it and began to cry uncontrollably and fell to my knees with my hands covering my crying eyes. Mattie came running up to me as did others.

"Are you going to be okay Scott?" Mattie asked me as she hugged me softly.

"How could I not be?" I responded.

Chapter 7
30 Years Later…

We walked down the sidewalk holding hands like we had done for the last 30 years. 30 years of many times a week, week after week, month after month, year after year and today was no different.

Mattie's hand felt amazing! I stopped a few times to bring it to my mouth so that I could kiss it gently. She smiled each and every time.

"Come on old man, you keep stopping for hanky panky, we'll never get to lover's lane," she scolded me quietly and lovingly.

"It'll be there when we get there," I responded, also quietly and lovingly.

Once there, we sat there for awhile, holding hands and kissing and I asked her, "What do you think about the last 30 years of us together?"

"What do I think?"

"Yes, what would your life have been like, with me not in it?"

"I am so very glad I didn't have to find out and I don't want to even think about it. Scott, I would never want a life without you, not for a second. You are the greatest man I have ever met. Women love you and even men love you, my mom and dad loved you. All these people loved you, but you were mine. I have you heart and soul. You were always mine from our first week together.

I could not have a better husband than you, nor a kinder man. You know how many times you kissed me in these 30 years? I've counted every single one of them," she said softly.

"Really?" I queried.

"Gotcha Ichabob!" She yelled excitedly.

"At least one million times I figure conservatively," she said.

"Add to that thousands of sexual encounters, tons of hugs and squeezes and you just about broke every world record possible for showing you love me," she said to me while looking into my eyes.

"How could I ever imagine a life without that? And you?"

"I love you so very much my darling, you have made these last 30 years as wonderful as they could be and have been. I am so very glad that I met you and fell in love with you and that you asked me to marry you and spend our lives together and it's not over by a long shot," she stated happily.

"I feel the same way my little Murgatroyd sweetheart," I said in a whisper.

"Come here you!" She exclaimed, "And let's add to that one million!"

And she kissed me long and hard as we sat there on the bench in this amazing Lover's Lane Park, that was renamed the Mattie & Scott Lover's Lane Park by the town some 29 years ago.

After we were sated, we began the long walk back to Mattie's place (yes I still call it that) where we were to have dinner guests soon.

Once home, Mattie and I went to work in the kitchen, preparing the dinner for our guests. Friends of ours all these 30 years.

"I'll get it!" I said upon hearing the knock on the door.

Mark and Maria walked in and as usual the hugs and kisses were flying about the house.

"You both look great," I said to them.

"How are the kids?" Mattie asked from the kitchen nearby.

"They are doing wonderful, talked to them both this morning," Maria stated.

Mark and Maria got married soon after the incident like we did. She moved in and they set up house and their practice together, expanding it and becoming more than enough for this wonderful little town of ours. They had two children, girls, now in their late 20's and both becoming medical doctors like their mom and dad. The kids plan on living elsewhere and practicing, since they deem it unnecessary to have more than two doctors in Hillsboro. However, the kids come home every chance they get and even help at the clinic when they are in town. Quite a beautiful family they turned out to be.

"Have you ladies picked out this year's scholarship winner yet?" I asked them both.

"Not yet," Maria answered.

"We whittled it down to two girls, we need a little more time to pick the winner," Mattie said to us all.

"30th year this will be awarded, Scott," Mark stated in astonishment.

"Yes, it was worth every penny," I responded.

The four of us sat down and ate and drank, I even pulled out my birthday tequila Mattie bought me, the $150.00 bottle good stuff. We all talked for a couple hours, enjoying each other's company so very much, like we have all these years.

"Scott's feeling a little melancholy today, our 30th anniversary," Mattie advised our guests.

"Not melancholy exactly," I said, "But amazed."

"What do you mean?" Maria asked me.

"I can barely remember my life before I came here. It is like I have lived two lives. Two very different and opposite lives in so many ways. In my first life, I barely remember the pain, of which I lived with constantly and tried to master it and block and deny it in my life, mentally and physically," I stated.

"We remember," Maria mused.

"And I don't miss that old life of course and those memories that I used to carry, I just can't believe I survived it," I said quietly, "And I don't remember them in detail, in fact I don't remember them at all."

"Those experiences and helping people in spite of them made you who you are and started you on this better path you have taken and are taking still," Maria said to me and the others, "I for one am glad you lost those memories and demons."

"But today, it really hit me," I said to them.

They looked worried.

"How lucky I have been these last 30 years. I am sitting at a table with three of the greatest people I have ever met in my lifetime. You know how many people I have met? And you three are the cats' meow. The best of the best and my tequila drinking buddies!" I exclaimed proudly.

"Mattie is as stunningly beautiful as the first time I laid eyes on her. In fact she became more beautiful to me every day I have had the pleasure to know her. Her smile makes me melt as it always has and her wit keeps me laughing, and her touch is magical and reaffirming and loving as a silly old man as I can hope for. In other words, today it hit me –wow!"

"Not that I haven't been grateful and thankful and loving and appreciative all these years, I tried my best to do that every single day, but the magnitude of these last 30 years is blowing my mind today. Words may not describe it well, but I'm trying to tell you three, that I love Mattie with all my heart and soul, always have and always will and my soul today, right now, is 10 times its normal size, it is so happy!" I laughed out in glee.

Mattie came over and hugged me and kissed me and squeezed me and told me she loved me with all her heart.

"Layoff the tequila old man," she told me and Mark and Maria laughed out loud.

"It's not the tequila sweetheart, it's you!" I explained.

Maria asked what else was going on with me today, she said, "Scott you seem a little more than your normal self today, because of your anniversary?"

"We have an anniversary tradition each year," Mattie told Maria and Mark. "We read each other's book about the incident; after all, the fair incident brought us together."

"What books?" Mark asked.

"We both wanted to write down our version of events to have for each other for posterity but also to help keep us focused on each other, since we were determined to love each other and spend the rest of our lives together, so we wrote them and we read them both each anniversary," Mattie stated.

"What are they called?" Mark asked.

"Scott's book is called, 'Mattie & the Yellow Dress.'"

"And Mattie's book is called, 'Mattie's Diary,'" I replied.

"Would you both like to read them?" Mattie asked them.

"Absolutely, we would love to read them," Maria shouted softly, having learned a thing or two from Mattie all these years.

Mattie went to the reading table and grabbed both hard cover books and brought them over and handed one to Mark and one to Maria for them to inspect.

"Take them home and bring them back as soon as you are done reading them, but read Scott's book first then mine, his is more detailed, all that cop training and experience documenting stuff," she said softly.

We finished our meal and talked some more about kids, work and our lives and then after bidding themselves gone, we were alone, Mattie and I.

"You locking the door or want me to do it?"

"Race you?" And we ran for the door, locked it together and walked hand in hand back to the bedroom, and after awhile, fell asleep in each other's arms like we had done so many thousands of times before.

Chapter 8
Mattie's Diary

I noticed the parked white VW beetle with Arizona plates and the attached older motorcycle as I was crossing the street towards the diner. I was going to pick up my usual cup of coffee and head down to the fair set-up and I wanted to be ready for the full day of hard work ahead of me.

Once inside, Carol told me a stranger wanted to talk to me about volunteering with the set-up of the fair. I walked over to him half expecting an idiot to answer me, thinking, what stranger would volunteer to help?

I asked him what he wanted and unexpectedly he answered, "I wanted to see if your eyes matched the rest of you," and I laughed out loud.

After a little chitchat and him showing me his retired police officer badge we agreed that he would meet me down at the set-up area after his breakfast. I left the diner never expecting to never see him again, chalking it off to him flirting with me.

A short while later, there he was. So I put him to work figuring once he started to work too hard he would pack up and be on his way out of our town. Surprisingly, he worked his butt off with the guys, they seemed to like his sense of humor and I sat down with him at the end of the day to have a beer with him. I couldn't figure him out at all. So I wanted to try. He thanked me in advance for sitting down with him and I didn't understand what that even meant.

He explained it to me that his career as a policeman showed him so much death and pain that he always wanted to say thank you in advance to people, in case he didn't get the chance to. Scott tried to explain why he wandered around the country looking for things to do, people to help, something about how his cop career took its toll on him mentally and I didn't understand but he was cute, a hard worker and he liked beer and tacos so I figured he couldn't be that bad and he did show me his cop retirement badge, so I figured he must be safe.

I was interested to see if he would ask about me or just talk about himself. Well, he did ask about me, then I wasn't sure if I wanted to tell him, but then for some reason I did. I told him of my happy life, my wonderful life in Hillsboro.

I asked him to stay at my house and use my guest bedroom, since he hadn't checked into a room yet in town, but first I wanted to see him clean and maybe even naked, so I took him over to the community bathhouse for a shower. His night bag was bright yellow and I asked him why and he said something weird and not understandable again, he said it was his favorite happy color and it made his slumped soul sit up straight. I didn't ask what that meant; I would save that for later.

I didn't want to just drop him off there, so I thought I could get him undressed if I was to wash his clothes. I told him to give them to me and I just stood there. If he would have told me to leave or turn around, I would have, but he simply undressed in front of me and handed me his dirty clothes and I couldn't help but laugh at his red underwear.

Wow, Scott was good looking! Even though he was dirty from working and sweating all day and his clothes showed it, he looked great, muscular and he looked like he could tip over a car if he wanted to. And he was not lacking in the man department, let's just leave it at that.

So I started washing his clothes as he took his shower and when he came out I handed him his towel and clean clothes. It was fun to watch him dry himself and dress himself, but I kept my hands off, at least for now.

I took him to my house and we drank some tequila and talked a little for about an hour then I showed him off to his spare bedroom and I passed out in mine. It was a long day setting up the fair.

The next morning I took him some coffee and woke him up and even kissed him once, just to see what he would say. He thanked me for the kiss and thanked me in advance if it came true that I would do this every morning. I laughed out loud again, he made me do this a few times in less than 24 hours that I knew him. I would watch this to see if this is a fluke or if this is normal with him.

Before we went back to the fair set-up area, I asked him to talk with me some more about his past. He told me that every single 911 call left him with some trauma and after 20 years and thousands of those traumas he suffered nightmares, restlessness and no peace, so he was traveling the country looking for love and peace and happiness. He said it was not working after 9 years of traveling and searching and he might not have happiness and peace and love in his future.

I promised him those things and off we went to the fair. I don't know why I promised those things to him, someone I didn't know at all, but something about him made me do it.

Back at the fair set-up and did he work! Every time I looked up, he was lifting something extremely heavy, carrying it somewhere and helping the men. He never stopped working, he never complained. He worked and got sweatier and dirty and never stopped. After about 8 hours, everyone was exhausted and ready to quit for the day, the fair was tomorrow, so anything we needed to do to finish the set-up could wait until then. I was about to ask Scott if he wanted to get some dinner at the diner, when he asked me if I thought the kids would like a ride on his classic motorcycle. I told him yes and for the next 2 hours, he gave every kid, every woman and man that wanted a ride on that wonderful classic motorcycle of his, a ride up and down Main Street. He smiled and laughed the whole time as I kept setting up the next rider for him.

Finally it was my turn and he asked to take me on a longer sunset ride, to which I gladly accepted. He apologized for his dirty white t-shirt and he said he could never make it to the end of the day with the t-shirt still being clean, I told him he was silly. As we drove, I wondered to myself how this man could do all these things if he was broken inside, how he could be so caring and think of others and be so nice. I told myself I truly do not understand all the things he told me.

I showed him where to drive and he was wonderful to hug, even his dirty t-shirt, as we rode to the sunset overlook not far from town. Once there we sat on the dirt ground together, he took a small blanket off his motorcycle for us to sit on, we talked softly about the day and how everyone worked so well together and he told me that he could tell that everyone loved me greatly. He told me how beautiful I was, his word was, "Gorgeous," and I thought no one has ever called me that I and I liked it. I told him I was a princess and he laughed with me.

We sat there for awhile and then we drove back to town. Along the way I was thinking a lot as I hugged him harder this time as he drove and I made my decision. Once he dropped me off, I told him to spend the night with me again and I went into my house. A few minutes later he walked in with his clean clothes and I called him from my bathroom.

He walked in and I was naked standing there and I told him I was going to take a shower with him if that was okay and he thanked me in advance rather excitedly.

Here was this man, who I knew could break me in half if he wanted to, he was so strong and formidable, but he was also gentle and kind. I still didn't understand his mental issues, but they couldn't be that bad with him the way he was and what he showed me these last two days.

I never wanted to leave the shower with him. I never had that much fun in a shower in my entire life, I only left the shower to get him into my bed and was I glad I did so, he made me feel like I have never felt before, he could go forever I believe and he seemed to truly care what he did to me or me to him. I think that two hours went by in 15 minutes, I have never lost time like that in my life, and I never felt that way in my life and that is all I remember until the next morning when I awoke.

I was up first and got up to make coffee for us. I began to worry if Scott had any nightmares last night, since he said they were always constant in his life. I wondered if he had any last night after spending time with me. I decided to wake him up and give him some coffee and test my theory. I watched him for awhile until he started to stir then I walked over to him with the coffee. I asked him if he had any bad dreams last night and he said no and that he dreamed of me and clouds and I knew he was talking about my soft bed and comforters and I laughed out loud again! I was so happy I could make him lose his nightmares for one night, I was so happy!

I kissed him and told him I had breakfast ready for him, I made him my favorite huevos ranchero with my salsa and he ate it all up! He loved my cooking as far as I could tell and he thanked me many times for cooking for him.

He was so very gracious. I kissed him across the table for a long time and I never wanted to stop.

I didn't know who this man was across the table from me, in my house, but I was glad he was here. After breakfast I told him we should get dressed and go to the fair, it would be a long day and I told him I had a surprise for him.

When I returned I was wearing my bright yellow dress for him and he smiled more than I have ever seen any man smile. It was more than a smile, I didn't understand it, but I knew it was more. He said it made his slumped soul sit up straight and again I didn't understand what that meant, but I decided to wait for more explanation another time, there was no time now.

Once at the fair he walked with me, holding my hand the entire time as we went booth to booth and ride to ride at the fair checking with everyone, making sure everything was ready and okay for the opening at noon. There were no big problems anywhere on the fairgrounds, except Joe backed his ice truck into one leg of the Ferris wheel. Scott and I and lots of the men folk checked the Ferris wheel and none of us saw anything out of place and the men were going to test the wheel to make sure it was safe.

Scott and I then proceeded to enjoy the fair and visited every single booth and ride, spoke to more than 100 people at least, was on the receiving end of lots of hugs and kisses and Scott got handshakes too. He said it was proof that everyone loved me and I told him it was because I was a princess. We laughed so much everywhere we went, he smiled and kissed me and squeezed my hand and I was so very happy. This went on for a few hours and instead of tiring out I felt more energized with every single minute. Scott too, I could see and it made me wonder what he truly meant, what could possibly be broken or hurt inside of him?

He was wonderful and I was lucky to be with him right now and he looked so strong and nice in his bright white t-shirt and jeans.

Then we heard terrible screaming coming from the Ferris wheel area. We ran over as fast as we could, I had no idea what we would find. The Ferris wheel was stopped, tilting to one side, full of kids in each basket and they were screaming, men and women were screaming at the foot of the Ferris wheel and I was looking all around when Scott grabbed me by both shoulders and kissed me. He then told me what to do and I understood him. I asked him what he was going to do and he said he was going to give me time to do all the rest and I understood him but I didn't, but I started yelling louder than others and told them all what to do.

I lost sight of Scott and ran up to various people and told them to evacuate, to save others, get everyone away from the Ferris wheel and the booths and once I had enough people running to do those things and I could see that they were being done, I ran over to the Ferris wheel and told the operator to go the normal speed unloading the kids and that is when I saw Scott.

My heart exploded right there and then. Scott was standing under the beam by the broken leg of the Ferris wheel and I could see him holding it up so that it couldn't fall down any further. I did not know how he was doing it, but I quickly thought, if anyone can do it, it would be Scott. I saw the veins in his neck pounding, I could sense his body being crushed, it tortured me but I had work to do. We didn't have much time, if only Scott could give me time to save everyone I thought and ran off.

I grabbed a few people and explained emptying the east parking lot of people and cars and to do it quickly, they ran off to do it. Having completed those three tasks Scott told me I now stopped not too far from Scott and talked to everyone that passed near me and directed them to safety. It only took a minute or two and everything seemed done. The parking lot and the fairgrounds were clear of all people and cars.

The Ferris wheel was down to the last of four baskets with three kids inside it. I saw as the wheel turned Scott's body was being driven down, but he never went down, he held it in place. I do not understand how he held it up, this Ferris wheel had to weigh a few tons overall and even his leg of the Ferris wheel must be at least a quarter of that and now more since it was leaning on top of him.

I saw Scott looking all around as he stood there and he seemed peaceful which I thought was odd. In fact I think I saw him smile like he was proud of us all.

Once all the kids were off the Ferris wheel and everyone at the fair was completely safe from the upcoming collapsing Ferris wheel and I didn't have to help save anyone else, I broke down crying, almost hysterically as I walked towards Scott.

There was no way I could save him, no one could save him, but I was going to try anyway. But Scott stopped me in my tracks. He waved at me to stay back and asked me quietly to not endanger myself for him. He knew no one could help him, he knew all along. He knew when he walked over there and braced the leg. How could anyone do that? I just found Scott, how could he leave me? This is what I was thinking, selfish of me and he snapped me out of it by saying he thought today was the day he would have a clean t-shirt the entire day. How silly of me.

We saved everyone except him. There would only be one death tonight and it would be Scott.

Then he was quiet for a few seconds. The weight of the Ferris wheel was pushing him down I could see. He couldn't hold it much more than a few seconds more. I wondered what he was thinking about just before he was to die in front of me. I never felt so helpless and I was glad it was hard to see him clearly through all my tears.

Scott then took a deep breath and said these words to me and I learned what he was thinking exactly before he was to die, he was thinking of me and he said, "Mattie, thank you for everything. I am so very glad to have met you. Thank you for wearing that gorgeous yellow dress for me, it gave my soul strength for this today. I love you Mattie." And he disappeared and the Ferris wheel collapsed. My heart exploded and I fell to my knees and I cried from the bottom of my heart.

There was so much dust flying around and after about 10 seconds or so it settled and there was Scott standing in the ruble of the collapsed Ferris wheel and I could see he was not okay. I got up to my feet and began to run to him, he took a few steps in my direction and fell down and when I got to him he was out cold, in fact it took me a awhile to make sure he was even alive, I could not get a pulse with all the dust and dirt but I saw his right shoulder bleeding and it was pumping out blood, so I knew his heart was beating and I yelled for help.

Many men ran over and grabbed Scott up carefully and at my direction we carried him to Doctor Sanchez's office and he let us in. The nearest major city and hospital was over 2 hours away and Doctor Sanchez said he had to stop the bleeding before he could be transported by some of us.

Scott was passed out cold and I explained to the doctor what had happened at the fair. He seemed perplexed and not able to believe what I was telling him and he asked me, "He held up the tilting Ferris wheel? That must weigh several tons." He shook his head and he was for the next two hours in disbelief as he worked on Scott and as I and the others in the room regaled him on the sequence of events and how everyone was saved except Scott.

I helped the doctor with a few dozen stitches in Scott's right shoulder and we didn't even give him any numbing shots since he was passed out completely and was not reacting at all with each stitch. I cleaned up Scott with a sponge bath and cut off his clothes and helped the doctor with his portable x-ray machine and we worked and worked and Scott never even moved. I kept wondering if he was having bad dreams and nightmares, I didn't want him to have nightmares.

The doctor was even more perplexed and made some phone calls to the hospital. He shared his results with them and they concurred with his expert opinion that Scott did not need to be transported to their hospital, unless something else cropped up.

Doctor Sanchez told us all in the room that Scott's vitals were all normal and shouldn't be. His blood pressure and heart rate were perfect. He said Scott should be crushed and dead, but again he was not. He was not reacting to pain as if he were blocking it somehow. He found no head trauma on Scott and the bleeding was easily stopped on his shoulder and Scott was not bleeding internally and that he truly didn't understand any of this at all.

He told us all that none of this made any sense, the incident at the fair and this man lying on his table right now. He was silent for a few moments and said, "It's not his time to die, that's all it can be, it must be."

I asked the doctor if I could take him home to care for him and he said yes without hesitation because Scott would need 24 hour constant care until he regained consciousness, someone had to watch for changes in Scott's progress and he knew I could do that and especially since I had a vested interest in Scott, from what he heard tonight from me and the other townsfolk in his office.

A few of the men then carried Scott over to my house and placed him in my bed and the all night vigil began. I was not alone, I had several friends and neighbors stay with me and many others quickly brought food and drink over to my house and everyone was quiet but making phone calls to their families and friends and checking on each other and telling of Scott's injuries and location.

All night long and the next day, over 50 people stopped by to take their turn to watch Scott and take care of me. I was exhausted, I called my parents to tell them of everything and I broke down crying, I couldn't stop and I remember falling asleep in someone's arms and hugs, but I wanted them to be Scott's arms and they were not.

Mid-afternoon, about 20 hours after the incident, I awoke to a lot of noise coming from my bedroom and a few people came running up to me to tell me Scott had come to and he thought he was in heaven. I ran in and my heart exploded again, this time with happiness and love for him. I rushed over and kissed him and squeezed him and I never wanted to let him go. This man who was willing to die for me and the children and my friends and neighbors.

He said hello and called me beautiful and I asked him if he had any bad dreams and he said no, just of me and floating in clouds. I thought even near death, he was thinking of me. I told him I would give him love and peace for the rest of his life and he thanked me in advance, that silly man. My silly man.

Later that evening the doctor stopped by to check the dressings on Scott's shoulder and check on Scott. This would be the first time Scott actually met Doctor Sanchez in person and they bantered back and forth in a good way. Doctor Sanchez had the x-rays and a folder with him and he told us that unbelievably Scott was going to be okay and most probably fully recover. I was elated and relieved and Scott noticed my reactions. After the doctor left Scott asked me to sit with him and hold his hand and he consoled me and made me laugh again with his corniness and outlook on life. He was a weirdo for sure, but a good, kind, caring weirdo.

Right on cue, the door rang and lots of people came in with food and drink and lots of hugs and crying and laughter and everyone was very glad to see me and especially Scott as he laid there in my bed. They tried to hug him and shake his hand but I asked them not to, so as to not move his stitches around. I saw a couple kids sneak a hug with him but I pretended not to notice. They were all so wonderful and they stayed for a short while and left us alone again.

Scott seemed a little perplexed as to what just happened and I told him to get used to it, that it would be the same every day until he was back on his feet, the townsfolk would take care of us both with food and drink and anything else we needed. He said something about what if we didn't like the food and I laughed out loud, locked the door and crawled into bed to make love with him, shoulder or not.

I slept soundly all night long, not much as a caregiver huh? Sleeping while my patient lies next to me, but I guess I was happy and exhausted and I held onto Scott's left side all night long. In the morning he told me he was up all night in pain and when I questioned him about not waking me up he said he was taking care of me for a change and he wanted me to sleep peacefully which I did. I felt bad and he told me not to, saying there was nothing I could have done anyway.

We dressed and went for a walk in town to loosen him up a bit and it worked. I gave him a tour of the town and he held my hand the entire time. He told me what he was going to say at the trauma counseling meeting tonight, but again I didn't understand exactly what he meant about me and the others being a hero and not including himself. Once back at the house we ate and we sat on the couch talking for hours it seemed, then we fell asleep on the couch, spooning, as he kissed my neck. It was wonderful.

Awhile later we awoke and got dressed and walked over to the auditorium for the evening trauma session put on by Doctor Mark Sanchez and his girlfriend Doctor Maria Snyder, who lived in a nearby town and who was a psychologist besides a medical doctor.

Scott went up on stage like it was a second skin to him. He was a polished public speaker, but his caring and concern could be seen on him, not just heard. He spoke of the incident and heaped lots of praise on everyone in the auditorium. He called us all heroes and life savers and that he was proud of us. I knew I saw that in his smile at the time of the incident.

And I saw his calmness during the incident, even though he was about to die and he explained to me and to all of us in the auditorium he was always prepared to die, he didn't fear death and this time he was going to do it for us, people he liked and loved, especially me. By now I was crying. I was thinking who was this man? How could someone so calmly give up their life to save others? Why wouldn't he have just stood there doing nothing or something else that wouldn't kill him in the end? I did not understand.

Scott was praising us and especially me in a wonderful speech, telling us all that we all lived through it and that is all that is truly important, yet he almost died to make that happen I thought to myself. I felt sorry for him in that he lived so many years always prepared to die every single day when he went to work, I truly felt sorry for him.

The more he talked the more I wanted to make sure he never had a bad dream ever again for the rest of his life. The more he praised me and the others, the more I pledged to myself to take care of him for the rest of his life and mine. He didn't know it yet, but he was mine and I would cherish him forever.

He spoke for few minutes and afterward every single person in attendance went to sign up for the trauma counseling and that speaks for itself. Doctor Sanchez and Maria didn't think too many people were going to sign up for the sessions, but now they had their work cut out for them.

As Scott walked off the stage I noticed he felt uncomfortable with all the applause and love being given by the crowd. He walked over to me and then we were bombarded by the crowd of people all hugging and kissing and thanking us. I could see his uneasiness up close this time and I told him I had something special waiting for him when we got home alone. This made him smile and made him forget his tension.

I thought here was man ready to die without so much as a whimper yet he didn't want someone clapping for him and what he accomplished. Add this to the growing list of what I didn't understand these last few days. I hoped to find out someday soon I thought to myself.

Once the meeting was over my parents walked up and surprised me and they told me they were sitting in the back of the auditorium and couldn't believe their ears. Scott told them everything said was true and especially about me and the four of us walked home together and ate and drank at my place for awhile. Mom hugged the wind out of Scott, so

I told myself I would have to do better and my dad just fell in love with Scott immediately.

Once they left, I wanted to let out the heat and boiling inside of me, I locked the door and shut the blinds and Scott was mine for the next couple hours, there would be no bad dreams tonight for him, let's just leave it at that.

The next morning Scott was up and dressed first as I awoke to him with a great cup of coffee in his hands for me. His kiss was tender and I loved having him wake me up. He told me he has several errands to run and said he would tell me later all about them and then he asked me for my yellow dress. I couldn't understand why he would want it, but I told him he could have it.

He kissed me for a few minutes and I almost begged him to stay and forget his errands, but I had to go work at the Senior Center for a few hours anyway. He asked me about a lover's lane in Hillsboro and I told him we did have one and we made a date to walk there sometime later today. I was very excited.

Off he went and I dressed for work and off I went. Several hours later he appeared at the Senior Center and the old ladies just loved him! He kissed them all on the cheek, talked with them and they all wanted to go to lover's lane with him for some necking! Scott is incorrigible! And we all laughed out loud.

We walked the 3/4 mile to the lover's lane park holding hands the entire way. We stopped a few times for hugging and kissing and we finally made it there. We sat and kissed and Scott felt so very good in my arms. As we walked back to my place Scott told me of all his errands this morning. Evidently Scott has enough money to never work again if he doesn't want to and all this since he retired at age 44. His cop pension and the selling of his house made this his reality.

He gave a lot of money to strangers in town and to the two doctors and then he tricked me in telling him I love him to his face, not in mean way, but in a loving way and I was glad he did. Then he told me he put $5,000 into my bank account because he cared for me and wanted to thank me for caring for him. Add this to my growing list of mystery stuff about him. I was thankful and told him I would show him how much I love him, just wait and see.

We returned to my place and made love again and I never wanted to stop. A knock on the door came, not long after we did and Scott rushed to answer the door while I got dressed. I could hear a lot of people that Scott let in and realized it was my friends and neighbors with food and drink again and when I walked into the kitchen area I saw that my folks were with them. I heard Scott tell them all to stay as long as they wanted and not rush off and they stayed two hours.

During those two hours everyone had the greatest time visiting with Scott and me, as we all ate and drank and laughed and some cried and everyone was exhausted as they left, as were we both. As we sat on the couch looking at each other we figured it would be two hours before the doctors both got here for supper and our first private trauma counseling session and we both couldn't get back to my bed fast enough.

Around 6 pm both doctors arrived and we all ate from the unlimited supply of food that my friends and neighbors had given us. Once full, we began the counseling session. I had the feeling Scott didn't need the session but he wanted me to be all right with the incident and stress and therefore he made it happen for us. Maria began a question and answer volley with Scott and he became upset and I asked to stop for the night and just visit with them. Scott asked to focus all the help on me and that he was not savable. I really didn't understand that statement and wanted answers now.

We dealt with me for awhile and the doctors thought I would be more than fine in the long run because my personality and with Scott by my side, an expert in trauma. We then decided, because Scott agreed to it, to delve deeper into his mental issues. Scott wanted a ten minute break to gather his thoughts and we went outside and he told me his slumped soul could no longer stand up and that his soul was crippled and damaged, maybe beyond saving and repair. I understood more, but not much and didn't know if I looked forward to the next hour or two or not. But I would do anything for Scott, so I decided I would listen and help him anyway I could, not only tonight but forever if he would let me.

We went back inside and to describe as astounding what happened for the next hour of Scott talking nonstop, without breathing and spouting things that the three of us had never heard of, read about, or could even conceive would be an understatement.

His ego never came out while he talked as he explained in great detail that pain and thousands of traumas have destroyed his soul and that he had no love of his life to help him live with all those pains all those years and that he became a machine instead of a man, emptying his mind of all thought, to survive the 20 years, all the while getting better at helping people along the way.

He described, and we all agreed, the many great traits of a great man, himself, but without saying he was the greatest cop who ever lived or even with not wanting accolades for his hard work and efforts helping people. He told us of a desire to no longer be a machine but wanting to be a man, loved by somebody, not for doing good deeds for others but in spite of them. He wanted to matter to someone and find love and peace or die while saving someone and gain eternal piece. Like a Viking or something I thought (Scott is Norwegian he told me earlier).

Scott never said he was owed love and peace and that he could not share his traumas with anyone in this world for fear of hurting them too, he only wanted peace and no more nightmares one way or another. And thus his traveling and searching to save himself or die trying.

I was crying off and on without any control of myself and I saw both the doctors doing the same and trying really hard to control themselves, but I could see they didn't understand everything Scott was telling us and that made me feel better, just a little bit.

Scott described in great detail the fact that every single day he went to work, he could die, never coming home to anyone or anything again. If he did live through the day, then most certainly there would be pain associated with the many 911 calls and victims and that he had no outlet once he was home, other than to turn himself off like an unplugged toaster, were his words. Then tomorrow do it again. And again and again for 20 years. I could not imagine such a life of pain.

He described not being afraid of death, even welcoming it, yet not being suicidal. He called himself a machine and expendable and willing to die to save someone. I am sure none of us understood this at all. He told us he was not on the same level as happy humans and that basically he could die and he felt, unlike me, he would not be missed by anyone other than his parents. But then he said his soul didn't understand this at all and wanted love and peace or to be released from his body by death.

He said his soul was crippled, bent over, unable to stand up at all and that it talked to him all the time, unrelenting in its desire to be released and freed from its captivity inside him. He said he could keep it in check while being an unplugged toaster, but he could not do that anymore and thus his traveling trying to find peace and love to save himself.

He told us in great detail of his professionalism in the fact that he always prepared for an emergency. He described how he watched me for two days and knew if the need arose he had a field general in me. At this I remembered him grabbing both my shoulders, kissing me and giving me guidance in what to do to save people the night of the incident. It wasn't an accident he did this, he was prepared to save people, no matter how much we laughed and kissed and walked around the fairgrounds, this fact was amazing to me I thought.

Then he did what he does, he took no credit for doing what he did and gave it all to me. He told us the reason he could do what he did, giving me and the others all the time we needed to save everyone at the fair was because of me! He said all that I did with him the last two days and the fact that I wore that silly yellow dress for him, his soul stood up for the first time in many years and that he didn't think it was possible.

He said he could have held up two Ferris wheels as if one wasn't enough! He said if I wouldn't have been there with him and wearing that yellow dress for him and crying for him as he stood there under the leg of the Ferris wheel that he couldn't have done what he did. And that dead and injured people would have been at the fair.

In closing, Scott said to us, "I hope Mattie is the one to make me nonexpendable and give me peace and love," to which I vowed to do just that.

We both slept the entire night through without stirring and woke up together and coffee had to wait a few hours, we had some smooching to do. When we were done and just lying there, I wondered what Scott would be like today, after last night's exhausting soul bearing extravaganza.

As he poured me coffee he called me sweetheart and asked if I minded and I told him that he could call me anything and he quickly asked, "Murgatroyd?" to which I was sorry I said, "Anything," but laughed out loud none the less. He was back to his normal weirdo self, the great kind. He then asked to teach me some SWAT sign language stuff and I said sure and he proceeded to teach me the "1-2-3 I love you" code. I asked if SWAT guys do this for real and he said of course not, but he wanted to teach me this so that no matter where we were he could tell me he loves me.

Just then the doctor knocked at the door and invited us both to the auditorium at 3 pm this day for our second trauma counseling session and he stated it would be different than last night's session. We both agreed and he left and we had 5 hours to kill and we did it with lots of kissing.

Once at the auditorium for the session, Scott amazed us all with great detail about how Maria and Mark were a couple, even though they were not demonstrative about it in public. The three of us were amazed and then Scott said he also saw their picture in Mark's office, which confirmed his theory.

Then Scott amazed us all again spouting just about every fact about my life to the three of us. Stunned faces on all three of us and Scott busted out laughing and said he learned most of it from my dad the other day when everyone was over to visit for a couple of hours. We all laughed out loud. Scott sure knew how to make people laugh and entertain them, even though he hid his demons away and took less credit for his abilities than he could have.

This trauma session went much nicer than last night's and Maria said they would be sorting out for years all the stuff Scott told us. Today's session was more question and answer and Scott was very sweet in his talk about me and others and I found myself not crying as much as yesterday. We even had smooch breaks for kissing and all four of us truly enjoyed that.

Scott talked about me and love and peace and even told Maria he fell in love with me before the collapse of the Ferris wheel. Maria asked him to explain more about his all powerful soul and the difference between that and adrenalin.

He said that everyone's soul is all powerful. He said his was crippled and broken with no hope. He said he was willing to die for me and all the others because they were important to me. He said he did it all because of me and the life I gave back to his soul and him and it was okay if he died, but it was not his time.

He told us in so many thousands of words, he proved to us in those words that his soul was all powerful that night and maybe I had something to do with that power and if so, I was glad. I made a vow to myself to never let his soul go to a slumped position again. Never. And I was eager to hear what the doctors had to say on the matter and how we all were going to prevent this from happening to Scott.

Scott made me cry again when he talked about being a machine and expendable and that he had no hope to save his soul, but when Maria asked him if he could become nonexpendable and find love and peace with me, he said yes immediately and my heart swelled up with joy.

Once the questioning was over the doctors both told us that I would be fine with the incident and that with my help Scott would get better every single day for the rest of his life, or so they believed. They told Scott that with me and time his soul would be doing cartwheels someday because his demons were limited in number and he wasn't adding to them since he retired and they should disappear with time and with all my love and caring. I also thought to myself, I would make sure he had no more bad dreams forever.

We slept great that night and in the morning I decided to sit on top of Scott and I didn't need him to be awake at first for me to do it, although he soon woke up smiling and that added to the pleasure. We spent a few hours in bed and then got up for some breakfast and he said he had a couple errands to run this morning, only about 30 minutes or so and that once back, he would love to walk with me to lover's lane. I told him I would be waiting and with a wonderful kiss he left.

Upon his return I met him at the door and hugged and kissed him, I missed him so much those 30 minutes. He told me Maria and Mark were going to join us to go to lover's lane and they showed up an instant later. The four of us began our walk and my neighbors asked where we were going, I told them and they joined us. As we walked the ¾ mile to the park, by the time we got there about 40-50 couples had joined our group, which even had some kids too. I was amazed at how many people joined us, but it was an amazing week so I just chalked it up to that.

We all walked back to our respective places and I couldn't wait to get Scott alone again at my place. The doors were locked and the blinds shut and for the next two hours I was in heaven. I never wanted to leave my bed again. Seriously.

However, we had to get up and start getting ready for the town party at the auditorium. Mark and Maria called for the party I guess, to celebrate our good fortune and the town caring for each other. But first I wanted to take a long shower with Scott and I thanked him for the very best week of my life and he said he could do this forever and I told him I would take whatever he would give me for however long he would. I love this man I said over and over to him and to myself.

Scott dressed in black slacks he ironed himself and the brightest white button up shirt I have ever seen. He looked fabulous and I grabbed my favorite red dress and he loved it too. We walked over to the auditorium and noticed the town was packed with cars, more than even the fair had and a couple hundred people were in attendance. We received lots of hugs and kisses and praises and again I saw Scott fighting against them and I told him to be gracious while I stared lovingly into his eyes.

Once inside he met with the Mr. Buchannan the banker, received some envelopes from him, then Scott joined Maria, Mark and I on the stage. Scott announced a $10,000 a year annual scholarship for a young woman in Hillsboro because he said Maria and I were great examples of amazing women and he wanted to ensure more of us in the future. I couldn't believe it.

Next he announced that Maria was moving to our town permanently to live with Mark and that he was giving them $25,000 to build up their clinic to double its size to accommodate two doctors instead of one. Wow. I was crying pretty hard by now, but this time it was a happy cry.

Then it was my turn. Scott called me up on the stage next to him, over to a cloth covered something and all the while he was telling everyone there how wonderful I was, how I was a true hero and life saver and not only did he love me but the town of Hillsboro loved me. He read me a plague and took off the silk sheet to expose my yellow dress framed in glass, and I thought what a sneak he was, that is why he wanted my dress and he told me over 100 people that were at the fair that night signed the dress for me.

To thank me for saving them and to tell me I was loved. I read a few names on the dress and I broke down crying. Scott held me and told me he loved me and after a few minutes I was okay.

Everyone was eating and drinking and talking, laughing and crying and happy and exhausted, but invigorated at the same time. I felt a lot of different emotions that afternoon in the auditorium. I looked at Mark and Maria and they nodded to me and I asked Scott to go outside with me to do some smooching and he readily agreed. I had to get Scott outside so that Mark and Maria could gather everyone inside the auditorium and teach them quickly the SWAT hand code for 1-2-3 I love you.

About 10 minutes later Maria came outside to get us and Scott said he was going to take his cake back from Maria since she stopped us from kissing and I scolded him.

Once inside about 300 people were standing in place, in front of the stage and I walked Scott up to the "X" which Mark taped on the floor. I told Scott he was done talking and it was my turn. I addressed the crowd and gave the very best speech of my life as far as I am concerned. I talked about how we all had each other for support but for 20 years Scott had no one to support him, however, Scott had us now.

I told everyone that Scott was sent to us somehow and I was glad and made them look to their right and to their left and imagine who could not be here today because if Scott was not at the fair that evening, some of us would be dead and injured. I could see the gasps in the crowd and many people started crying and others smiled in agreement. I asked them to Thank God for sending Scott to us.

Then in front of everyone I promised to take care of Scott and love him and cherish him for the rest of my life. Kiss him, hold him and love him with every ounce of my being and I would do this gladly for the man I love. I told everyone I never met a man like Scott and I was going to keep him forever.

I said other things to praise Scott and I turned around and saw that he was crying pretty hard, maybe partly because he never wanted praise like this, but more I thought because I was telling him everything he wanted and needed deep down inside to hear, that I was his, now and forever, and that I would love him with all of me.

I then walked up to him and told him to stay put and walked off the stage into the center of the front row with my folks and Mark and Maria. All eyes were upon me and I raised my right hand as high as I could. Everyone in the crowd did the same, even the 4 little old wheelchair bound ladies from the Senior Center. I then held out one finger and the crowd followed me, then a second finger and the crowd followed and then a third finger. We all held them up high for a few seconds and then I touched my heart as did the others.

Scott fell to his knees and covered his crying eyes so much so that I thought we hurt him somehow. I ran up on stage to him as did so many others and I hugged him and asked him if he was okay, and he said, "How could I not be?"

I knew then he would be okay and mine forever.

To order more copies of this book:

Please go to www.lulu.com or to any major or minor bookstore and they can order it for you; either way in about one week you will have your copies at the bookstore or mailed to your address.